"*D*o you always get what you want?"

"Yes," he said.

RACHEL VAIL

You, maybe

The Profound Asymmetry of Love in High School

HARPER TEEN

An Imprint of HarperCollins*Publishers*

Harper Teen is an imprint of HarperCollins Publishers.

You, Maybe:
The Profound Asymmetry of Love in High School
Copyright © 2006 by Rachel Vail
www.harperteen.com

Library of Congress Cataloging-in-Publication Data
Vail, Rachel.
    You, maybe : the profound asymmetry of love in high school /
Rachel Vail.— 1st ed.
    Summary: Josie, a fifteen-year-old high school sophomore, is
smart, funny, and very much her own person, but when popular senior Carson Gold starts wooing her, she cannot resist his
attention.
    ISBN 978-0-06-056919-8
    [1. Identity—Fiction. 2. Interpersonal relations—Fiction.
3. High schools—Fiction. 4. Schools—Fiction.]
PZ7.V1916Yo 2006   2006000365
[Fic]—dc22   CIP
                                                    AC

Typography by Amy Ryan
❖
First HarperTeen paperback edition, 2007

DEDICATION

Audrey and Nick fell in love in high school. I was in eighth grade, Audrey's little cousin with braces and a bad perm, and from behind my books I watched them. They were the most glamorous couple I could imagine: both gorgeous, tan, athletic, easy-going, popular, and deeply generous. They were best friends, madly in love. And so they always remained. This book is dedicated to their daughters Lucy and Sophie, to Audrey, the strongest, bravest person I know, and in memory of Nicholas Psaltis.

One

AS SOON AS we rounded the corner I realized it was a mistake to crash, but by then it was too late to stop. A lot of the Beautiful People were at the party, even on the front lawn. Clearly not our crowd. Zandra, Tru, and I squeezed past the couple on the front porch, pretending not to notice who it was: Carson Gold, the hottest senior guy, shaking his head at a gorgeous girl who was trying not to cry. I rolled my eyes at Zandra after we were clear. "Another one down," I whispered. She laughed and shoved me forward. I stumbled over the threshold, into the party.

We shouldered our way through the crowd, pretending we were looking for someone. As we were passing a couch in the living room, a couple who'd been making out on it stood up and rushed away, apparently in search of a room. Zandra, Tru, and I plopped down instantly in their space, next to another making-out pair. We were wedged in pretty tight, with Tru's skinny thigh in its short skirt pressed against the hip of the oblivious girl beside her, but we smiled at one another triumphantly: We had scored seats. We sat back, pulled off our mittens, unzipped our jackets, and looked around.

Parties are our favorite spectator sport.

Not much was going on. We shifted positions and kept scoping.

"So," Tru started. "What would you say is the single most important thing?"

"In life?" I asked. "No contest. Chocolate."

"Books," Tru countered.

"True love," Zandra said. "Do you think Emelina is here?"

"No way," Tru said. "She never goes to parties where Carson will be."

"Ugh," I groaned. "This is why I vote for chocolate. It's yours, it's wonderful, you gobble it up, it's gone. Good-bye. Maybe you feel a little guilty, but at least chocolate doesn't hang around at parties you want to go to. You know?" Their obsession with Carson Gold was beyond me. I mean, sure, he's gorgeous, in a generic all-American way. And even I watched sometimes last year when he and Emelina Lee glided through the halls, holding hands. They whispered to each other in corners and kissed in the stairwells. But then Emelina got accepted to Princeton early and when she went to visit for the special weekend, she fell in love with a college

2

boy. She dumped Carson that Monday morning in the school parking lot. Nobody could believe it, least of all Carson. The rumor shot around that he had almost punched her, but at the last second punched his new car instead. Zandra and Tru dragged me out to the parking lot during lunch later that week in search of his white Mazda, to check. Sure enough, there it was, a dent right on the roof near the passenger door: proof. My two best friends were practically electrified with the passion of that. What can I say? I'm a pacifist. Punching your own car seems pretty stupid to me.

"Think he was dumping that girl on the steps?" Tru asked.

"Clearly," said Zandra. "He's still in love with Emelina, everybody knows it."

Tru nodded solemnly.

"Gag," I said.

"You don't understand romance, Josie," Tru said. She's been studying. She's read forty-seven romance novels, as research. Tru skipped first grade so she's a year younger than me and Zandra, and she looks about ten, especially with her braces and wire-rimmed glasses. She is trying to be less of a bookworm this winter, but I think her pursuit of romance is stressing her out way more than advanced calculus ever has. We like her just fine as she is, all serious and sincere and intense. But it's hard to convince her to stop trying to be less herself; she's on a mission.

"Neither does Carson Gold, apparently," I pointed out.

"Just because he's hooked up with half the senior girls doesn't mean his heart has healed," whispered Zandra. "Sometimes sluttiness is a sign of intense longing."

"Yeah?" I asked her.

"Trying out a new rationalization. What do you think?"

"Pretty good," I said.

Zandra is the opposite of Tru in a lot of ways—she's curvy where Tru is tiny, outrageous where Tru is timid. Zandra's hair has not been its natural color since elementary school, she's more street smart than academic, she has seven piercings, and as for experience with guys, well, Zandra has made out with a lot of guys, but never has had a boyfriend. As tough as she looks, what she really wants is to fall in love.

"Think about the way he used to look at her," Zandra whispered to Tru. "Have you ever seen anything so romantic?"

Tru leaned forward to talk around me. "I know—as if he wanted to swallow her down whole."

"Ew," I said, sitting up behind them. "Like an oyster?"

Tru and Zandra clutched my arms as Carson Gold himself stalked into the room and stopped right in front of us. Sunk into the couch, our heads came up to about his hip. The girl from the porch flung herself at him, her arms grabbing him from behind.

"But I love you, Carson!" she pleaded. "I thought you loved me!"

What a nightmare. We sunk deeper into the back cushions to watch.

"Don't do this," he murmured, gently disentangling himself from her tentacle-arms.

"Carson!"

"Shh." He looked at her with soft pity, not like he wanted to swallow her whole.

Her hands went to her hair and she pulled, squeezing her eyes tight. A groan escaped from deep in her throat. I was so embarrassed for her I had to look away. I pulled my cell phone out of my bag, for something to look at, and text messaged my friend Michael:

BP'S SELF-DESTRUCTING HERE. YOU?

The girl plowed through the crowd like a guided missile toward the door, and I heard Carson Gold exhale above us. I kept my eyes on my phone, as my friends stiffened on either side of me. I was trying to work up some pity for the poor girl. I couldn't. I mean, she knew who she was dealing with, right? So why make a jerk of yourself over him? Or over any boy? Was he supposed to act like he was married to her just because they'd fooled around once or twice? Please, we're in high school. Hook up and move on.

Zandra and Tru both suddenly squeezed my arms tighter.

"What?"

"He looked at you," Zandra whispered fiercely.

"Sure."

Michael texted me back:

FRIENDS CRAPS TACOS HERE. COME.

"He totally did," Tru whispered, nodding. "Right at you."

"Lucky me," I said. "You guys want to go to Michael's instead?"

"Are they playing craps?" Tru asked. When I nodded, she grinned. Tru's a champ at shooting craps, we recently discovered. She says it all boils down to figuring out what's most likely to happen, and something about how many ways there are to make eight.

We hoisted ourselves off the couch. "I'll call my dad," Tru offered, rummaging through her bag for her cell as we headed toward the door. "He'll be psyched. He got me a new book on probability this week."

On the way to the door we passed this guy Andrew, a junior I had hooked up with a while ago. He and I checked each other out, considering a rematch.

"Josie," Tru called from the door. "Come on!"

I shrugged at Andrew and spun around, right into Carson Gold.

"Ow," he said.

"Right back at you," I answered.

I went around him and caught up with my crazy friends, who spent the whole ride over to Michael's deconstructing the multiple possible meanings of "Ow" and envying my encounter with the great Carson Gold. Luckily, once we got to Michael's we started rolling dice, which moved us on to more interesting subjects like whether or not luck actually exists.

Two

TUESDAY MORNING AS I was spinning my combination lock, Carson Gold leaned against the locker next to mine.

"Hi," he said.

"Hi," I answered.

"I'm Carson."

"Oh," I said. As if anybody didn't know who he was. I knelt down to get out my books, thinking *Wow, I guess he is literally giving every girl her moment in the sun.* I wondered if he keeps track on the school directory, checking us off.

He leaned over me and looked at the schedule I had taped inside my locker, in my one moment of organization back in September. I could feel his leg nearly bumping my head so I stayed crouched while he looked. "Josephine Dondorff?"

"Josie," I corrected him. I stuffed what I needed into my backpack.

"Hey, I have seventh period free, too."

"Wow." I zipped my backpack and stood up. "We must be meant for each other," I said, and slammed my locker shut.

"Must be," he said, then stopped smiling. "Do you believe in that?"

"In what?"

"Fate." He looked so searchingly into my eyes, I had to take a step back.

"No," I said, and started clomping off toward my homeroom.

"I do," I could swear I heard him say, behind me.

At lunch, my friends were practically panting for details. "Did you really say that?" Zandra asked. "Meant for each other?"

"Yeah," I said for the fourteenth time. "We were just kidding around."

"'We.'" Zandra shrugged. "Maybe Tru is right."

Tru looked up from her book, surprised. "Right about what?"

"Tru thinks you're in love with Michael."

Tru clamped her lips together.

"Because I kissed him good night after the craps party?"

"No, just . . ." Tru took a deep breath. "You just seem, so, comfortable together."

"We are," I said. "Like I am with you guys. I'm not in love with you either, sorry to say."

"You don't kiss us like that," Zandra pointed out.

I laughed, and so did she. "It doesn't mean anything," I explained. "We're just friends."

"You sure?" Zandra asked.

"Shouldn't I know?" I chomped a big bite out of my sandwich.

Suddenly Zandra's green eyes flicked to a point above my head, alarmed. I turned around, still chewing. There was Carson Gold, looming above me. Usually he and the other Beautiful People were tossing a ball at each other in the courtyard during lunch, or going out to the pizza place. Not hanging around inside the cafeteria with the alternative-type tenth graders.

"Josie," Carson said.

"Carson," I said, trying to swallow my overlarge mouth-ball of hummus with all the fixings.

"What are you doing seventh period, today?"

I shrugged, swallowed, and said, "You, maybe."

Zandra's mouth opened wide. Tru dropped her book.

Carson smiled. "Excellent."

When he walked away, my friends shrieked and grabbed me. Honestly, I could hardly believe it myself.

Three

AFTER SIXTH, HE was at my locker. He asked where I
wanted to go. I suggested my house, and he said okay. My
parents are never home. I showed him around the main floor
and then in my living room we started kissing.

He was gentle and tentative at first. We were standing near
the TV. He is much taller than I am so he had to lean way
down and I had to stretch. After a minute, I pulled away and
asked if he wanted to sit down on the couch. He nodded. We
sat next to each other there for a moment, staring forward at
the blank TV screen, but then he put his arm around me and
started kissing me again, softly. My left arm was kind of stuck
between us so I picked it up and touched his hair with my fingers. His hair was thick and really soft. I tangled my fingers
into it as I leaned back against the couch pillows. His right
hand traced the bottom of my jaw as we kissed and kissed.

Whoa, I suddenly thought. *What am I doing?* I'm not a prude but I am also not interested in going much beyond kissing with anybody. My parents are not home and this is a guy who punched a dent in his own gorgeous car when he was denied something for maybe the first time in his life. So what should I do? Because he's a senior, seventeen or maybe eighteen, maybe he will expect me to go a lot farther. I don't even know how old he is! What have I started here?

I tried to think of something not completely babyish to say. I pulled my head slightly back from his, to get more oxygen to my minimally functioning brain. He tapered off his kisses slowly, adding one light, lingering final peck on my lips. I opened my eyes. He was smiling sweetly, almost apologetically at me. "What?" I asked him. My voice came out sort of hoarse.

"I have to get back to school for basketball practice," he whispered.

"Oh," I said.

"I'm sorry."

"That's okay," I assured him. Phew.

"I gotta go," he said, standing up and smoothing his hair back into place. His long legs took about four strides to get to the front door. "I'll call you."

I was still kind of foggy, indented into the couch. The door closed as I was answering, "Yeah, okay."

Everybody knows what "I'll call you" means. It means good-bye. Nothing more, nothing less. I sat there smiling at the neatness of the whole encounter. Phew.

I was still half-lying on the couch in a daze when Zandra called me, the minute she stepped out of school. "So?"

"What?"

"Did you fool around with him?"

"Yeah." My face was smiling all on its own.

"And?"

"Even better than he looks," I said.

"Wow," Zandra said. "How far did you go?"

"How far do you think?"

"Made out."

"Yup."

"That's good," she assured me. "That's my new leaf I'm turning over: the take-it-slow leaf."

"Sounds good," I told her. She turns over new leaves weekly.

"Was he a good kisser?"

"Really good."

"I knew it!" she screamed. "Did you ask him about Emelina?"

"No!"

"Why not?"

"Well," I started. "One, it's none of my business. Two, it would be a little awkward to ask about his ex while his tongue is in my mouth, right?"

"True," she agreed. "That's a good point."

"Three, obviously he's still hot for her, everybody knows that. So why ask?"

"You're jealous!"

"Jealous?" I snorted. "Of course not. I'm not his girl-friend or anything. We hooked up. It was fun. The end. What's the big deal?"

"It's Carson Gold! You can't tell me you're not in love with him."

"I'm totally not in love with him," I said.

"Then you are the only girl in the whole tenth grade who's not."

"Okay."

"Maybe tomorrow he'll ask me," she said dreamily. "I'd do him in a heartbeat."

"You should," I recommended.

As expected, he didn't call that night. Zandra and Tru were watching me the next morning for signs of trauma but there weren't any.

"Why would there be?" I asked them. They shook their heads knowingly and headed out to the courtyard for their morning people-watching time. I slumped down next to Michael to listen to the new song he had composed. He's a really talented musician, especially on keyboards. I love watching him play. "Souvenirs," he called the new song. When it was done I took a deep breath. "The music is beautiful. . . ."

"Yeah. The lyrics. I know. I just mumbled in some filler until you have time," he said. He's not great on lyrics but that's where I come in. We're a good team. Someday we may be legends. "But you like the sound of it?"

"It's really good," I told him honestly. "Kind of, haunt-ing."

He grinned. The gap between his front teeth is so cute. "Good."

"So I have to think . . . souvenirs, huh?"

"Just seemed like . . ."

"Uh-huh," I agreed. "Definitely. Yeah. Let me hear it again. I want to get that bridge melody in my head."

He gave me one ear thingy and took the other, and we sat there listening to the song over and over until the bell rang for first period. We hauled ourselves off the cold floor.

"Seventh period, back of the library?" I asked him. Michael has seventh period free, too.

He nodded, on his way down the hall.

I went to class thinking I am such a slut, two different boys in two days—because usually if Michael and I get going on a song, we end up making out a little. I decided not to think about that. The circumstances were totally different; the Carson Gold thing was just a weird, fun aberration. All through my morning classes I wrote and crumpled up song lyrics: *indentation on my couch pillow, a souvenir of you. . . .* No. *It wasn't meant to last, but at least I have my souvenirs. . . .* No. *Postcards fading on the wall, the summer dimming into fall, we didn't know we had it all . . .*

I got to lunch humming the bridge part, still not satis-fied. Zandra and Tru were already at our table. "Michael was just in here, looking for you," Zandra told me. "I told him he could hang with me but he took off. Does he hate me?"

"You know he doesn't." I unwrapped my lunch.

"What is it then?" she asked. "Do I have boy-repellent on?"

Tru said, "They sell that?" and picked up her book. She's determined to read every book on the American Library Association's Top 100 Books before she graduates high school, without missing a single week of *People* magazine. It's like a double major.

"I think my mother secretly mixes it into my shampoo," Zandra said, and continued scoping. "I haven't hooked up with anybody in two weeks. I may have to dye my hair again, to overcompensate for my unfulfilled horniness."

Zandra is planning to dye her hair every color of the rainbow during her high school career. She's done red and orange already and is currently on yellow, a very pale yellow that was almost white, which I think is her best so far. "Your mother is freaking out now," I said. "I can't wait to hear her reaction to the green."

"It will be a thing of beauty," Zandra predicted. "I think she secretly loves me, though, despite how she acts."

Without looking up from her book, Tru put her hand on Zandra's shoulder.

Michael slipped into the seat across from me. "Looking for you. How's it going?"

"Not there yet," I said.

"I had a different idea for the beginning," he said. "So don't—it's more of dee-da-da, dum-dee-dee-da-da . . ."

"Okay."

He shook his head and put his ear things back in. He closed his eyes and his face relaxed completely. I smiled at him and started to eat.

Zandra gave me a hard elbow in my side.

"Hey," I complained, but then I looked up and saw Carson Gold looming above us.

"Hey," Carson said back.

I chewed and swallowed. How does he always catch me with my mouth full?

"What are you doing seventh?" he asked, with that killer smile.

"A friend," I answered, with my mouth still slightly full. I swallowed again. "A favor for a friend."

He looked shocked. "Really?" he asked.

"Really," I said, and wiped my mouth on my napkin.

"You're mad I didn't call last night. I just . . ."

I gave him a look. "No." As if I would *ever* be that fool girl chasing him around screaming *Call me! Don't you love me? I love you!*

"So then why don't you want . . ."

"I just have other plans today." I took a sip of my water and noticed Zandra, beaming up at him. "Do you know Zandra? And this is Tru." Tru looked up from her book, surprised. "This is Carson."

"Hi!" Zandra said. Tru didn't make a sound, just kept staring at him.

Carson didn't look away from me for a second. "You sure?"

"Maybe tomorrow," I said. Luckily Michael still had his eyes closed and his music on. Not that he would've cared, really—we have no commitment to each other or anything, of course—but still. Even though we always tell each other who we hook up with, because it truly has nothing to do with our friendship, I don't know. We don't shove it in each other's faces. And I hadn't told him yet about Carson Gold. "Okay?"

"Yeah, tomorrow." Carson smiled. "Maybe," he added, and walked away. So he had the last word. Well, hooray for him, he got to end it.

"Are you crazy?" Zandra asked.

"I had plans," I said, continuing to eat.

"Why not, you know, rain-check the old standby?" Zandra whispered.

"What," I whispered back. "*Sorry, Mikey—I got a better offer?* I don't think so," I said.

"I told you," Tru whispered. "Love."

"I have standards, that's all." Both my friends made dubious faces, so I added, "Well, okay, they're low standards, but I have them."

"I say you are definitely either in love or nuts," Zandra said. "Or maybe both."

"Maybe I'm just a good person," I suggested.

Zandra and Tru considered that; they shook their heads and both said, "Nah."

"Either way," Zandra said. "If you're done with Carson, can I get him next?"

"There's a sign-up sheet in the gym," Tru told her dryly, then turned to me. "I can't believe you just turned away Carson Gold."

I shrugged. "Easy come, easy go."

"You are definitely the coolest person I know," Zandra said. "I would've done him right here in the cafeteria."

"Why do you think he wants Josie?" Tru said, going back to her book. "If you want a boy to like you, you have to feign disinterest, like Josie's doing."

"What do you mean, *feign*?" I asked. "I *am* disinterested."

"In what?" Michael asked, opening his eyes.

Zandra and Tru turned to me, too, daring me to answer.

"In . . ." I started. "In, in, in being ordinary."

"No worries," Michael said, and closed his eyes again.

Four

THE NEXT MORNING when I got to school, Carson was leaning against my locker with his arms crossed over his broad chest and an irresistible smirk on his lips. Just as I had wished and not expected him to be. "Hello, again," I said.

"Today," he said.

"Okay." I smiled back.

"Really?"

"Meet you by the back exit after sixth," I said, and zipped over to Zandra and Tru's lockers to tell them Carson Gold was coming over again. Their mouths dropped open in shock, and they did some bowing and chanting of "we are not worthy."

"You must have done something really awesome in a past life," Zandra said on the way to lunch, which got us all into a whole argument about reincarnation. When he got bored of past lives, Michael passed me one of his ear buds and I tried to concentrate on the revision we'd done of his song. It was a challenge. We had worked on it really hard all afternoon, and then made out for about half an hour. I still hadn't told him about Carson—I had kind of figured it had been a once-in-a-lifetime weird thing, and tried to convince myself it was irrelevant, anyway. But here I was, about to hook up with Carson again: Carson, Michael, Carson. Yikes. I had never done anything like that before. Part of me felt like no big deal, it doesn't hurt anybody for me to kiss two different guys, very different guys, who are both great, and anyway there's nothing wrong with kissing. But part of me (my stomach, mainly) felt like maybe this is not so cool. But what could I do?

As promised, Carson was waiting for me by the back exit. I had walked there telling myself maybe he wouldn't show, maybe he'd stand me up, to punish me for blowing him off the day before, and maybe that would be the end of it and really, I'd been stressed for nothing. But no, there he was, waiting for me, watching me with his laser beam eyes. It felt like a spotlight. I couldn't tamp down my grin at all. He bent down and kissed me, lightly, right there in the hall. I followed him out to the parking lot.

On the way to my house I put down the windows of Carson's car, turned the radio all the way up, and sang along. He touched my leg and smiled. I was in a seriously great mood. It was warmer out than it had been in weeks, the sky was crisp January blue, the music was rocking, and I was about to do some good fooling around with the hottest guy I'd ever laid eyes, never mind hands, on. He parked in my driveway, and as I got out of his car I touched the dent on the roof with my fingers. We walked up to my house not talking. I unlocked the door. Instead of going straight to the living room, though, I dropped my jacket, sweater, and bag in the hall and went to the kitchen. He followed me.

"What are you doing?" he asked.

"I'm hungry." I love anticipation. I wanted to hold off the moment of colliding with him for another minute.

"I have basketball practice at 3:30."

"Ugh." I knelt down beside the pot cabinet, to keep from looking at him. "Just thinking about basketball practice exhausts me so much I think I might have to go lie down on the couch and watch TV to avoid getting a cramp."

"I like your couch."

"It likes you, too. But first I need a snack. You want some egg salad?"

He laughed. "You're really turned on, huh?"

He should only know. "I make the best egg salad you've ever had. Secret ingredient and everything."

"Mmm," he said. "My favorite food."

"Egg salad? Really?"

"No. Secret Ingredient."

While I filled my mother's heavy red pot with water, he stood right behind me and touched my waist with his fingers. Giving in a little, I leaned back and rested my head against his chest, dancing a little to the music still in my head. "I love these pots," I told him.

"You love . . . what?"

"Seriously. They're so beautiful and heavy. My mother bought a set of three of them last year. She has never cooked anything in them, of course, but they are the best, hard to get; you had to be on a wait list to get the set of three pots in red, so of course she had to have them. She was on the phone with the store manager all week, cutting in line."

Carson started kissing my neck. I set the pot with six eggs in it over a medium-high flame on the stove. I couldn't hold off anymore. I turned around. We made out for a while, until Carson asked, "What were you doing yesterday?"

"Yesterday?"

"Seventh period."

"I'll never tell," I said, kissing him some more. Yesterday? I didn't want to think about Michael right then. It felt like a betrayal on too many levels.

"You like to torture me," Carson said.

"It's my hobby," I said. "Beats performing at birthday parties."

"You perform at . . ."

"Don't get any kinky ideas," I said, unbuttoning a button of his shirt. "Children's birthday parties. I'm a clown. You know, magic, games, the whole thing."

"Okay." He shook his head. "You want to go into the living room?"

"Let's go upstairs," I said. I walked ahead of him, skipping the squeaky step. We got to my room and didn't bother with the light. When we heard the first noise we were on my bed and not all my buttons were buttoned anymore, either.

"What was that?" I asked.

We listened, still as statues, him up on an elbow, his face right above mine. Nothing. I shrugged and he did, too, and we went back to each other until we heard two more clonks, one after the other. Now we knew it wasn't our imagination.

"Somebody here?" he whispered.

I shrugged again, only one shoulder. My parents never come home during the day. My mother works in the city, in advertising, and my father sees his sore-footed patients until six.

The next clonk was a loudie. Carson and I dove off the bed and hid behind it. He crouched, buttoning his shirt fast. That made me smile because it was like, uh-oh, what if bad guys have broken into the house and see me with my shirt unbuttoned? Though I have to admit I rearranged myself, too.

"Do you think we're being robbed?" I whispered.

He nodded gravely, then crawled over to my closet and opened it.

"Did you want to borrow something more formal to wear for the robbery? I'm not sure I have anything in your size."

"Shh," he whispered. "Don't you at least have a tennis racket or anything?"

"You think they came here looking for a doubles partner?"

He turned around quickly and gave me a look, then whipped a Wiffle bat out of the mess.

"Wow," I said. "You jock-type people really are single-minded, aren't you? Uh-oh, we're being robbed. Let's play ball!"

Clonk-ka-junk-ka-jzzz, from downstairs.

"It's for a weapon," Carson whispered.

"You're gonna hit them with a Wiffle bat?"

"What else you got?"

"Um . . ." I looked around my room. I'd never particularly noticed before how weapon-free it was, though I do consider myself strongly anti-violence. "A pillow?"

"Exactly," he said.

"Maybe we should call 911," I suggested.

"Where's your phone?"

"Oh," I said. "Downstairs."

There was some very aggressive clattering. It sounded like they were coming closer. Carson stood up, with the bat cocked back. He looked very studly, it must be said, despite the misbuttoned shirt. "Stay behind me," he whispered.

"Can I just say that I never knew this about myself before, but weirdly enough this whole protective he-man thing actually turns me on."

"Josie."

"What?" I asked.

"Shut up."

I grabbed my pillow, just in case, so to speak, and tiptoed behind him around my mussed-up bed. "Maybe we should just hide in the closet."

He turned around, rolled his eyes, and kissed me. "Shh," he repeated.

I was going to press my point, because I was truthfully starting to get a little scared and hiding seemed like a much better plan to me than confronting real live burglars with a hollow yellow bat and a Minnie Mouse pillow, but then I decided maybe he was right and it would be a good time to shut up, actually.

Carson opened my door and slipped out. No way was I staying in my room alone, so I leaped out after him and grabbed the back of his shirt with the hand that wasn't already clutching my Minnie Mouse pillow, mourning all the things I would never get to do in my tragically shortened life.

By the time we got to the kitchen my heart was pounding and my nose was scrunching. It stunk. It was a mess. No bad guys, just eggshell shrapnel everywhere, and bits of egg, and a burned red pot. It smelled like somebody had died.

"Oh," I said, turning off the stove. "Oops. The egg salad."

Carson lowered the bat. He turned around and gave me

a goofy grin. "That's some secret ingredient, Josie."

"I'm full of surprises."

"Yeah," he said. "I see that."

"Help me clean up?"

"Sure."

I grabbed some potholders and brought the pot to the sink. When the water hit it, it hissed. I jumped back. Carson kind of caught me. I spun around.

"Were you scared?" I asked. "When we thought, you know . . ."

"No."

"Me, too," I said.

He blinked slowly, and smiling just a little, reached toward me. "Your shirt is buttoned wrong." He unbuttoned my shirt.

"Yours, too," I said, and unbuttoned his, too. Our shirts hung like that and we looked into each other's eyes. When he finally pulled me close, I could feel the pounding of his heart through his soft skin.

Five

CARSON WAS LEANING against my locker when I got to school the next morning.

"Hi," I said.

"Hi." He didn't take his eyes off me for a second.

"I gotta get my stuff in there," I told him.

"Your parents say anything about the smell last night?"

"Not to me," I told him. "They kept asking each other, 'Do you smell something?' 'Yes, I do. Do you?'" It was weird to try to have a normal conversation with him, as if we were friends.

"What would you have told them, if they asked you?"

"The truth," I said. "But they didn't ask."

"What's your combination?" Carson asked me, turning to my lock. It was kind of a personal question. I wasn't sure if we were close enough for me to tell him. Just because I let a boy undo my bra, does that mean I should let him into my locker, too?

"I'm not going to steal your chemistry notebook, Josie," he said.

"You wouldn't want it," I answered. "If you try to, though, I should warn you, I have a Wiffle bat."

"And a Minnie Mouse pillow," he said.

"Exactly. Twenty-five, six, thirty-three," I said, figuring, what do I care? I never have anything important in my locker anyway.

Spinning the dial, Carson asked, "Who else has it?"

"What?"

"Your combination."

Just because I've never given my combination to anybody before doesn't mean I never can, or that it means anything if I do tell somebody. "Nobody."

"So I'm your only one." He grinned at me.

"Well," I hedged. "Besides me."

He yanked open my lock. "I'm in," he said. "There's no getting rid of me now."

"Hey, do you have a dark spot on your eye?" I had never noticed it before, but in the midst of his wide hazel iris was a tear-shaped spot of black.

"That's my witch-eye," Carson whispered, leaning close. "My bio teacher, Mr. Garcia—did you have him?"

I nodded.

"He told me it was a witch-eye. He said I have magical

powers. So watch out—maybe I'll bewitch you."

"The bio teacher believes in witchcraft?" I shook my head. "What does that say about our science curriculum?" I couldn't help noticing some of the girls in my grade congregating at the end of the row of lockers, watching this. They really follow him around like a swarm. I dumped my morning books into my locker and excavated my chemistry stuff.

"Well?" Carson asked. "What do you believe in? Chemistry? Cold hard science?"

"Chocolate, books, and true love," I answered.

He smiled at me. "Me, too. At least chocolate and books. Love is a brat."

"Yeah. A brat?"

"Absolutely," he said, leaning against the next locker, his face close to mine. "Whatever you don't love, loves you. But whatever you love tends to kick your butt."

"You think?"

"Trust me," he whispered. "Stick with chocolate and books."

"That's been my strategy so far," I told him. "I was kidding about the true love part. It was a quote."

"Aristotle?"

"Zandra."

He looked perplexed.

"My friend. You met her."

"Okay," he said. "Chocolate, books . . . and fate."

"Fate? Nah."

"How about football?"

"I don't think so. Rock and roll?"

"Keep an open mind. Come over Sunday for the Eagles game."

"Um . . ."

"A bunch of people are coming over around three. We'll have some food, you know, hang out."

"The thing is . . ." I said, thinking, *I'd rather stick needles in my eyes.* I know the people he's friends with. Beautiful People. People who toss balls around in the courtyard at lunch instead of arguing about Ayn Rand. Players. Anyway, I was busy. "I have a party from two to four." I bent down to search for a pen in the bottom of my locker.

"Blow it off," he said. "Mine will be more fun. I promise."

"I can't blow it off. I'm working at it."

"So come straight from it. I'll save you a seat."

"Thanks," I said, standing up. "But . . ."

"Come on, Josie." He leaned close and whispered in my ear, "I really want you there."

"Yeah?" I asked, slamming my locker shut. "And do you always get what you want?"

"Yes," he said.

Six

"CARSON GOLD?" Michael asked, hooking leashes on Fluffy and Sarge. "Seriously?"

"That's what I'm saying," I said.

"The Golden Boy?"

"You know another Carson Gold?"

"Your mother must think she died and went to heaven. Captain of every team, president of every club . . ."

I shoved Michael, but added, "Able to leap tall buildings, blah blah blah."

Michael locked the door behind us. Every day after school he walks Fluffy and Sarge, then brings them home and brushes them, all for twenty dollars a week. I go with him sometimes, since Fluffy and Sarge live with Annabel and Tom in the house between my house and Michael's, on our little dead end, one of five dead ends in our development.

Michael is madly in love with Annabel. That's really why he walks the dogs, not the twenty bucks. "So what did he ask you to do exactly?"

"He wants me to come over to his house Sunday," I told him. "To watch the football game."

Michael laughed.

"I'm serious."

"You're not going, are you?"

I shrugged. "I'm doing a party right near his house, so I might stop by, after."

"In your clown costume?" Michael asked. "Carson Gold and his BP friends would enjoy that."

We watched the dogs sniff around the trees. Fluffy is very particular about her spots; Sarge will pee anywhere and everywhere.

"Forget it," I said. "How's the song?"

"In pieces."

"Should we work on it, after?"

"Maybe," he said.

By then we had gotten down to the dried-up stream in back of Dead End B. I leaned against the big, bare elm tree we carved our initials into last year. Michael unleashed the dogs, who chased each other around. Michael pressed up against me and we made out for a minute. That's what we always do when we walk Fluffy and Sarge. People sometimes think Michael and I are going out with each other, but we aren't. We're just friends who make out with each other.

Neither one of us wants a romantic entanglement; neither of us feels the typical high school need to be half a couple. We don't get jealous of each other and we're honest with each other; we've been friends since nursery school. Kissing just happens to be part of our friendship, that's all. I think if parents knew how many afternoons teenagers spent fooling around with their friends, they'd lock us all up until we turned twenty. But maybe I'm wrong. Maybe they did the same with their friends when they were young, too.

Usually we make out for a while but this time I pulled away. It's not that I didn't enjoy making out with Michael. I just wasn't in the mood. For the first time.

Michael looked at me all confused and maybe a little rejected.

"What?" I asked, defensively. "Even a nympho like me is entitled to be not in the mood occasionally, right?"

"Whatever." He shrugged and looked down, so his dark hair flopped over his face and I couldn't see his eyes anymore.

"I just, I have a lot on my mind today."

"He drove you home?" Michael asked. "That's why you weren't on the bus?"

"Yeah."

"After sixth or after seventh? Because I looked for you in the library, seventh."

"After sixth."

He turned away.

"What? He has seventh free, too. A lot of people do," I

babbled. "Remember back in like September, October, when you were hooking up all the time with Emma Barrett seventh period?"

"Twice." Michael patted his leg and the dogs came running. We started back up the hill together. "You were hooking up with him?"

I shrugged; he shook his head. Michael hates BPs.

"So you think I should blow it off, then?" I asked him. "The football party, I mean?"

He bent down to latch on the leashes. "Is he messing with you, you think?"

"In what way?"

"Forget it." He stomped away from me, up the hill.

"Hey." I caught up with him and grabbed his elbow.

"Think about it, think who this is. Carson Gold. How does he treat girls? And what do they look like, every one of them? How do they act? Right? Do you think he, or any one of his girlfriends, has ever had an original thought, or done an outrageous thing? What kind of music does he listen to? Whatever is 'in', I bet you."

"You are such a snob, Michael," I said. "The worst kind of snob, because you think you're above snobbery. What kind of music does he like? Give me a break. He happens to be a smart, interesting guy who invited me over to watch a football game. That's all. It's not a referendum on his character. Forget it, I never should've even mentioned it." I started up the hill by myself.

He yelled from down below, "I'd love to see you show up there as Tallulah the Clown. You think he'd even invite you in?"

"I told him I work as a clown," I yelled back. "And he thought it was cool, as a matter of fact. He's the one who suggested I come straight from the party I'm doing." We stared at each other, our hands on our hips, puffs of cold air exploding from our mouths.

"Whatever," Michael said, trudging up after me. "Do whatever you want. You're just abnormally stoked that he's cast his glamour rays on you, is all."

"You think he's too good for me? You think a guy like that would never actually like me?"

"No," he said. "The opposite."

"Meaning what?"

"Nothing. He likes you?" he asked. "I mean, *likes you*, likes you?"

"I don't know."

"Do you like him?"

I shrugged. "I hardly know him."

Michael shook his head. "If he . . . Watch out for him, that's all. I know everybody thinks he's perfect, so nice and, and catch of all catches . . ."

I had to laugh. "Catch of all catches?"

Michael's cheeks flamed red. "I don't trust him."

"Why not?" I asked. "You don't even know him. You're just judging him on totally superficial qualities. Isn't that what you always say is wrong with society, that people get judged by superficial qualities? Hypocrisy isn't confined to the Beautiful People, Michael. Hey."

I tipped his pointy chin up, so I could look into his face.

He pulled away. "All I'm saying is, if he's just playing you, I swear . . ." His voice cracked.

I grabbed him by the collar of his jacket. Michael and I are about the same height so I looked him square in the face, though he was looking down and away. "Hey," I whispered. I kissed him lightly on the lips and said, "My hero."

"Screw you," he answered.

I followed him back to Annabel and Tom's house. He took the brush from its shelf, put away the leashes, gave the dogs their dog treats and sat down on the step to the living room to brush the dogs. I hung back and watched. It's like a meditation with him, I think. Stroke, stroke, stroke. I watched Fluffy go into her getting-brushed trance. I wondered what it might feel like to have Michael brush my hair sometime, if he would be that steady, that gentle with me.

"Don't go."

"What?"

"I mean, do what you want," Michael said. Fluffy walked away, looking back at me over her shoulder, clearly annoyed with me for ruining the best part of her day. Sarge sat down at Michael's feet, panting and ready for his turn. "I just . . . Trust me, Josie. Don't go."

Unfortunately, I rarely do as I'm told.

Seven

AS I WAS ringing the doorbell, I had an almost over-whelming urge to run. I never have an urge to run (usually my urges are to nap) so I would've acted on it but I am slow even in sneakers, and in clown shoes I am likely to trip even walking. Well, I trip in sneakers, too. Diving into the bushes was not a possibility either, as his door is flanked by rose bushes. Also, I have dived into anything (it was a pool) a grand total of once in my life, an experience I prefer not to remember, never mind repeat. So I stood my ground.

Oh, hooray. In a close match, inertia wins over panic, and the crowd . . . the crowd? Uh-oh. Panic was staging a late comeback.

What the heck am I doing here? This has got to be the most foolish thing I have ever done. I am standing on the front porch of Carson Gold's house dressed as Tallulah the Clown because . . . why? Because Michael pretty much dared me to? That is stupidity itself. He dared me to take off my pants in kindergarten once, and I had the sense then not to do it. And now, ten years later, I am humiliating myself to prove what? And to whom?

Maybe Carson will just answer the door and smile, say, oh, great, you came straight from the party. He'll compliment my costume and ask me a question or two about how the party went, what tricks did I do, how old was the birthday kid, as he shows me where the bathroom is. Then he'll give me a fresh clean washcloth and some Noxzema. And some spare clothes to wear. Sure.

I am an idiot! What the hell am I doing here?

Maybe they didn't hear the doorbell and I could just sneak . . .

The door swung open just as I was turning away from it, panic having triumphed after all.

We stared at each other, Carson's mother and I. We'd never met before, but I knew who she was. She's in the halls a lot at the high school—PTA president or something, probably. She was in jeans and a light blue T-shirt, her hair pulled back in a ponytail and no makeup on.

"Hi," I said.

"Hi," she said.

"I'm a friend of Carson's."

"Really?"

"Yeah, I'm surprised about that, too, actually."

"Excuse me?" she asked.

"He invited me to a football party and, though I have forgotten why, here I am."

Carson's head appeared, over her left shoulder.

"Hi," I said to him.

"Josie?"

"Yup," I said. "I, I came, straight. Strangely enough."

Carson and his mom continued to stare at me, so I stared back. I had never before realized how alike they looked, how specifically alike, not just in the way that all very good-looking people look sort of alike, in that they are so symmetrical, and all healthy, good-looking, all-American people have that similarly scrubbed and vigorous look about them. Carson and his mom actually had similar facial structure, with their wide-spaced eyes and their close-to-the-head ears.

"Sure is cold out here," I said.

Carson swung the door open for me, finally. "Why are you . . . seriously, what's up?"

I wanted to go home so bad. "I was working. Remember? You said I should . . ."

"As a clown?"

"No, as an astronaut. Yes, as a clown. I told you I do magic at kids' parties." This was all going so very well.

"Uh-huh," Carson said.

"I told you I had a party today from two to four, and you said . . . I thought you . . . forget it."

"Carson," said his mom. "Why don't you invite your

friend in and shut the door?"

A crowd had formed at the end of the hallway. There were some adults and some kids. They were all staring at me.

"Carson," she repeated.

"Hello," I squeaked. "I'm Tallulah the Clown! Is today somebody's birthday?"

Nobody answered. Earlier in the afternoon when I asked that, twenty kids screamed out the name of the birthday kid. Unfortunately there were no birthday kids in the house, and no five-year-olds, either. I glanced up at Carson, who looked uncharacteristically awkward. "No?" I asked, in my Tallulah the Clown voice. "Wrong house, I guess!"

I turned around instead of walking into the house through the door Carson was still holding open. Despite my efforts at dignity, I tripped going down the front steps and my feet found themselves in a sort of extended race to catch up with my head. If I had been trying, I don't think I could have made a more perfectly clownish exit. Too bad that was not the effect I was trying to achieve.

I hurried down the walk as quickly as I could go, without risking further pratfalls, toward my bike, which was locked to his basketball hoop at the edge of his driveway.

"Josie," Carson shouted.

I turned around. He was standing on the front porch in his T-shirt and sweatpants, his ragg-wool socks scrunched down below. Damn. It is seriously unfair for a guy to be so cute. "The name's Tallulah," I shouted back.

"I thought you were coming to watch the game."

I cleared my throat and spoke strong and clear, this time. "I didn't mean to embarrass you."

"Yes, you did."

Did I? Was that my plan? Why would I want to embarrass him in front of his friends? No, that wasn't exactly it. I guess I was kind of a little bit hoping that seeing me show up in a clown suit, in full whiteface with a red ball nose, rainbow hair, and huge shiny shoes somehow wouldn't embarrass him.

I stuck my hands in my pockets.

"So?" he asked. "You gonna watch the game or not?"

"You still want me to?"

"Sure. Come in." He is a very well-brought-up boy, you gotta give him that. Unfailingly polite to his guests, even the ones who don't belong.

I clapped my hand over my mouth like I was shocked, and popped in the rainbow streamer packet I'd palmed. I pretended to start to choke.

"You okay?" he asked.

I kept pretend-coughing.

He ran toward me, across the soggy, cold grass in just his cute socks. When he got to me, he put his hands on my shoulders and asked again, authoritatively, "Josie, seriously. Are you okay?"

It occurred to me that he might give me a Heimlich maneuver and make me puke on his lawn, so I decided not to drag the trick out any further. I started pulling the streamers.

"Ew," he said. "Are you . . . What is that?"

I kept pulling, hand over hand, and the rainbow colors began streaming out of my mouth in a long paper garland. Carson backed up two steps, looking mighty confused. A crowd had gathered on the porch and was watching, so I did the whole thing I usually do, clowning around like I was even more shocked than they were, pulling and pulling, seven feet of rainbow streamers, unfurling out of my mouth. When I finished, I coughed the last little shell of it into my hand and shoved it in my pocket, and said, "Must've been something I ate."

On the porch, Carson's sidekick, Frankie Caro, started clapping. A few others joined in. I took a deep bow and Frankie's girlfriend, Margo Van Deusen, whistled for me.

Carson, on the other hand, still looked almost comically shocked. Since I was fairly sure it was the last time I would ever have the chance, I kissed him on the mouth, leaving makeup smudges on his unresponsive face. Then I jumped on my bike, rang the bell, and pedaled off, waving a merry good-bye to the whole A-list lot of them.

Eight

THIS IS EXACTLY why I am not romantic, I told myself as I rode home fast, flying. This whole crying thing, that's why. This whole, I-think-I-just-blew-my-chance-at-having-this-boy-really-like-me thing. I don't want this. I don't want any part of this.

I dumped my bike in the garage with all my supplies still on the back, and charged up the stairs to my room. I ripped off my wig, threw it on my bed, and yanked my costume down hard. Damn. I hate hating myself.

I pulled on some sweatpants and a zip-up sweatshirt jacket, yanked my hair back into a ponytail, and smashed my way to the bathroom. It's my own fault, I reminded myself as I layered cold cream on my face. What did I even want? What did I expect? Did I really think Carson Gold would see the girl behind the Tallulah the Clown getup as anything but a freak? Had I really become so gullible that I could con myself into believing he was really asking me to come straight from the party I was doing, so he could see what I do?

When will I ever meet that guy?

No, I do not allow myself to think like that!

I bent over the sink and scrubbed hard. I have always had a really strong feeling that out there somewhere is someone who would see me whole and wacky and particular, and would not just put up with all my personality, but would actively like it. He would encourage me. He would be somebody who doesn't enjoy the tasteful, neutral beige of my mother's decorating—he would be someone who likes neon plaid. Polka dots. Pink with red. I knew it would be a long wait; that's okay. I am a patient girl.

But I guess the truth is, I let myself hope a tiny bit that maybe, somehow, ironically, that person could possibly be Carson Gold. I lathered myself up with Cetaphil for the second round of scrubbing.

The thing about getting your hopes up is that it is a phenomenally stupid thing to do. There is no upside to high hopes. That ant with the rubber tree plant was delusional. Please. Think about it: You let yourself hope for a thing. Okay, so if you get it, then it's like anticlimactic: like, so what? I already pictured getting this thing I wanted, this boy or whatever, and here I am getting it. So no big deal.

I dried off and stormed down to the kitchen.

But if you don't get the thing you were hoping for, I continued inside my head, let's just say for the sake of an example a stupid, plastic, perfect boy's love, you are devastated and need to eat an entire pint of cookie dough ice cream immediately, which can lead to a horrible ice cream headache and also to dirty looks from your mother, if your mother is a person who thinks your worth as a human being is inversely proportional to your weight.

On the other hand, if you never get your hopes up, you can go through life considerably less battered. You have to protect yourself; it's just common sense. No animal would willingly, purposefully, put himself in a vulnerable position, right? So why would a supposedly higher-order animal like a human do it?

Right?

But that's what we do when we hope, I reminded myself as I scrounged through the cabinets for more to eat. When we hope, we set ourselves up. In the Greek myth, Pandora let *hope* slip out last when she opened her forbidden emotion-box, and the moral of the story is that *hope* was like the antidote, the compensation for all those bad feelings like fear and lust. I don't know, *fear* and *lust* seem like healthy emotions to me. They let the species survive. Hope, on the other hand, is a pointless emotion if I ever saw one. What good did hope ever do us? I think never expecting anything good to happen is a very healthy philosophy, and most of the time, I am proud to say, I am able to think the worst of most people and most situations. That's why life doesn't beat the stuffing out of me anymore. I have learned the trick.

But today I forgot. I messed up. I hoped. It's my own fault that today I am like the peach you would never pick at the grocery store, bruised and passed over and sad.

I was forced to eat the plastic bag full of Swedish fish I got in my party favor earlier in the day. You have to love a host who gives the clown a loot bag—and cash.

"I wish you wouldn't . . ." My mother, coming back into the kitchen, stopped herself mid-critique. She took a breath, then another. I ate a whole handful of Swedish fish at once. She looked away and started over: "I'm making flounder for dinner."

"You're cooking?" *If I were a kind person I would warn her to stay away from me right now,* I thought.

"Ew, please," she said. "I'm heating. I got it from the place with the sign, you know. Near that horrible gas station?"

"Sounds great," I said. Warning, combustible!

Her eyes lingered on the empty ice cream container on the counter. I watched her try to hold in her thoughts about my weight, my supposed lactose intolerance, my messiness—all the things that make her sigh when she looks at me, her little bundle of disappointment.

"New hairstyle?" she finally asked. "It looks kind of nice."

"No. I just washed my whiteface off."

"Ugh. Doesn't that stuff give you pimples?"

I shrugged. I was doing my best to hold all the bile in.

"You used to be so terrified of clowns . . ." she said. "Remember when you wet your pants at the circus, soaked right through my skirt, and I had to carry you out, screaming, with everybody staring at us?"

"Everybody's afraid of clowns," I said, finishing off the candy.

"So why in the world would you want to dress up as one?" She forced a smile, as an afterthought, as if she were just kidding around.

I rubbed my finger and thumb together. "I make fifty bucks an hour. There are very few legal ways for a fifteen-year-old girl to do that."

"Well, aren't you the berries," she said.

"I think so," I lied.

I could never explain to her the real reason I like being a clown, doing kids' birthday parties. She had never asked me why I liked it before, and this time it wasn't interest, obviously—it was criticism. Money she understands. Money is power, she once told me, when I was really young and she was depositing money at the bank. Money is power, Josie, she said; a woman needs to make money. She might have forgotten telling me that but I never forgot it.

"If you need money," she was saying, "all you have to do is ask me and I'll . . ."

"I don't need money," I said. "When's the last time I asked you for money?"

"Never." She fluffed her hair. "You never . . . I'm not criticizing you, Josie."

"No?"

"No. You seem so tense. All I'm saying is you would have a lot more fun if you didn't try so hard to be . . . different."

"Different comes easy to me," I said. What I could never explain to my mother is that although the makeup does in fact give me pimples and the wig is itchy and the parties are absolutely exhausting, I love it. It is so incredibly cool to transform myself into Tallulah the Clown. Just like Carson, she thinks I do it to embarrass her. Right, Mom—it's all about you. Not. And same to you, Carson Gold. Guess what, both of you? It's actually about me.

It's the magic that's like a drug, an addiction for me, and I don't mean the dumb tricks, pouring water into newspaper or pulling my stuffed rabbit, Hops, out of a mirrored box. I mean the real magic. Behind the clown makeup, I get to watch the kids' faces change—from fear, to wariness, to acceptance, to joy. Hiding under the fake hair, behind the bright red lipstick smile, I can reach them, and I can watch them overcome something, and see them believe in magic. As Tallulah, I get to be different—more fun, funnier, more confident, way more lovable. At the beginning the kids clutch their mothers' legs. By the end, they all want to hug me. Yes, it takes a lot of work. But it is the most worthwhile thing I do.

But it's easier for my mother to think it's for money, or

rebellion. Just like it's easier for Carson Gold to think I do it just to embarrass him. Fine. We're all free to believe whatever nonsense we need to, to get through the day.

"Forget it," Mom said, grabbing a Diet Coke and flopping into a chair. "I don't know why I even try."

I felt a little guilty then, so I said, "Neither do I." It wasn't her fault my day had sucked. This time. Also my mood was lifting a bit. I'm not good at depressed and angry. Also there was a lot of sugar coursing through my bloodstream.

"Mom, tell me the truth," I said, sitting in the chair next to hers and propping my feet on her lap. "Does everybody know the hokey pokey is really about love?"

She shoved my feet to the floor and scowled at me, but I could tell she was holding in a smile. I drive her nuts but I don't bore her, at least. "What are you talking about, Josephine?"

"All this time I thought it was just nonsense and wiggling. But then while I was working today I got to thinking, you know, you put your whole self in, you take your whole self out—that's what it's all about. That's got to be about love, right?"

"Well . . ." she paused.

"This is a good talk we've been having, Mom. Thanks. I think we should . . ."

A car pulled into our driveway. We both looked quizzically, if not suspiciously, at each other.

"Is that Daddy?" Mom asked me.

"Daddy is in the living room, reading the paper," I reminded her.

"Oh, yeah. So who's here?" She checked her lipstick in the microwave reflection.

"Probably somebody lost, making a U-turn," I said, jumping up to dance. "You turn yourself about . . ."

And then the doorbell rang.

Nine

"HEY," SAID CARSON when I opened the door. "You changed."

"I'll never change," I said.

Mom peeked over my shoulder. It was weirdly parallel to our earlier moment at Carson's door.

"Mrs. Dondorff?" Carson asked.

Mom pushed me to the side and extended her hand for Carson to shake. "Barb," she said. "And you are . . . ?"

"Carson," he said, shaking her hand. "Carson Gold."

Mom smiled radiantly at him. I managed to control my gag reflex.

"I was wondering if Josie could take a ride with me."

"Really?" I asked.

"Yeah," he said.

"Okay," I said.

Mom looked past him to his little white sports car in our driveway. Mom has been looking up little sports cars on the Internet for months; I've seen the sites she visits. I try to mentally condemn her shallowness, but what can I say? I love his car, too. It's a stick shift, it gleams, it's got red leather seats. Even the little dent in the roof had started to give me a little charge. Though I have not, will not, ever admit that to Zandra and Tru.

"Um," said Mom, sounding uncharacteristically uncertain. "Bill?"

"Hm?" answered my father, from behind the paper.

"Josie wants to go out."

"I brought home the new shoes for her, for her arches." I heard him standing up in the living room, shuffling his paper and lowering the footrest on his Barcalounger. "Josie?" he called. "Sweetie, I want you to wear these—your arches are really collapsing . . ."

"I thought maybe we'd get some ice cream," Carson added.

Before Mom could explain that I am both on a diet and lactose intolerant, and had nevertheless already consumed a pint, and before my father could make it to the front hall brandishing the latest in his long line of orthotically engineered shoes to combat all that is wrong with my feet, I said, "Sure, love to."

Pushing Carson back out the door, I grabbed my jacket off the hook and shoved my feet into the great old clogs that my poor podiatrist father wants outlawed.

"Don't you want to change or something?" Mom called after me.

"She'll never change," Carson answered, and followed me down the steps.

I settled myself into the passenger seat and buckled up as he backed out of the driveway. "Your arches are falling?"

"Turns out I am deeply flawed," I admitted. I considered saying I was sorry for earlier, for embarrassing him or whatever. I hoped maybe he'd get it, that admitting how flawed I am was sort of my apology. If I needed to apologize.

He shifted into first gear and checked his mirrors. "I like your hair like that," he mumbled.

"Like this?" I had forgotten I had a ponytail in. "Really?"

"You don't?" He shifted gears and kept his eyes on the road.

I shrugged. "It shows too much of my face."

"That's why I . . . what do you mean, too much?"

"My face is too flat," I explained. "It's too . . . never mind. You had a sudden ice cream craving?"

"I like your face," he said. "You should wear your hair like that more often." He pulled up to the highway entrance.

"Where are we going?" I touched the hair above my forehead, smoothing it down. He liked my face.

"Let's just drive awhile, okay?"

"Okay," I said. "You rescued me from my mother. No arguments. I'm just happy to be sprung."

He waited for an opening in the traffic, tapping the steering wheel lightly with two fingers of his left hand, then bolted out into the stream of cars, smoothly shifting as he accelerated. I watched his hand on the gear shift, his long fingers relaxed on the knob.

"I didn't mean to embarrass you," I stated. "That's not why . . ."

He shifted again, and released the knob. His hand drifted over and covered mine, on my lap. "I like your earrings," he said.

I touched one of my diamond studs, with my free hand. "Thanks."

"New?"

"No, old. I never take them off. They were my mother's grandmother's."

He smiled a little. "Cool. What was her name?"

"My great-grandmother's?"

He nodded.

"Josephine. I'm named after her. I'm supposedly a lot like her, which is apparently not a compliment."

"Why not?"

"She was a big crusader for women's rights, a doctor, the whole firebrand thing."

"I like her already," Carson said.

"She never took these diamond studs off. My mother got them after Josephine died, but she likes danglies. My mother, I mean. She was saving these for me, planning to give them to me when I turned eighteen. But I loved them. I wanted them. I convinced her when I turned fifteen I should have them, promised I'd never take them off, and eventually I guess I wore her down."

"You always get what you want, too, huh?"

"I don't know," I said. "I guess so. So far."

"So far," he repeated. "You have an interesting way of thinking."

I didn't know what to say to that so I turned on his radio, lowered my window and sang for a little while, but my heart wasn't in it, so I put up the window and turned down the volume with my right hand. My left was still under his, which was warm and heavy.

"Why don't you ever sing along?"

He checked his mirrors. "I can't."

"Of course you can. Come on. It's just talking, spread out. Everybody can sing."

"Not me."

"Really?"

"Trust me," he said, shooting a glance over at me.

Okay, that was even cuter than how he looks in his lacrosse uniform. He can't sing. And his palm was starting to sweat, discussing it. A chink in his white-knight armor. "Someday I'm gonna get you to sing," I warned.

"Never," he said.

We drove north for a while like that, until he suddenly downshifted in an exit lane and we took a sharp right, glided through a stop sign, turned right again, and parked in back of a gas station near the air hose.

Carson yanked up the emergency brake, turned the car off, and leaned over to me. Oh, so that's what he wanted. When he mentioned ice cream I thought he meant ice cream.

We made out for a minute.

"Josie."

"Yeah?"

"I don't . . ." he looked away, out the windshield toward the air hose. "Are you fooling around with other guys?"

"Not at the moment," I said.

"You know what I mean."

I unbuckled my seat belt, which had been strangling me, while I thought about how to answer. "None of your business," I said.

He turned to me. "I want it to be."

"Tough," I said. "You're fooling around with other people."

He shook his head. "It's Michael Addison, right?"

"What is?"

"Are you in love with him?"

"In love?" I was completely confused. "Michael is my neighbor," I said. "He's my . . . We're friends. We, I mean, I like him, a lot, but. Wait. I don't have to justify my friendship with Michael to you."

"So that's a yes. You're in love with him. Okay. But then

56

my question is, why are you messing around with me?"

"I'm not in love with him! Are you kidding? Why do people keep thinking I'm in love with Michael?"

"Other people think so, too?"

"No. They don't. Michael is like, he's, I mean, I love him. Sure. Of course I love him, he's been one of my best friends since nursery school. He's nice and brilliant and talented; we have a great time together, sometimes, although I have to say at some point today I considered going to his house and killing him slowly and painfully. But in love with him? That's a whole different thing. He's in love with somebody else, anyway."

"Who?"

"Her name is Annabel. You don't know her."

"Where does she go? Sacred Heart?"

"She doesn't . . . She's a . . . Who cares?"

"You're in love with Michael Addison but he's in love with somebody else? Is that it?"

"No," I said. "I am absolutely not in love. With anybody. Love is a brat, you said so yourself."

"But you are fooling around with him. Not at this instant, I know, Miss Lawyer, but recently, recurrently. Right?"

"What are you, like, the morality police? You have to be in love with somebody to hook up with him? Hello? I happen to know from personal experience you are not waiting until you get married to hook up with somebody."

"Is that what we're doing then? 'Hooking up'?"

"You didn't notice?"

"So you do the same stuff you do with me, with Michael Addison?"

"None of your business!" This was without a doubt the weirdest day of my life.

He slammed the steering wheel with the heels of his hands.

"What?" I asked him. "You're hooking up with half the school."

"No," he said. "Only you."

"That's a lie."

"It's true," he insisted. "I swear it's the truth. Since I first kissed you, Josie, I haven't done anything with anybody else. I haven't even thought about anybody else."

No way. "Really?"

He nodded.

"What about Emelina Lee?" I clamped my jaw shut. I hadn't meant to bring her up.

"It is totally over between me and Emelina," he said.

"Whatever," I said. "I don't care. I didn't mean to even bring it up. It's not my business."

Carson backed his seat up and turned toward me. "You have no idea, do you? You have no idea how pretty you are, how sexy. How smart and strong and independent and different you are."

"Different I noticed," I said.

"Me, too," he continued. "Do you know how much I, I, how much I like you?"

"Because I wore a ponytail?"

"Yeah," he said, rolling his eyes. "It's definitely the ponytail. It had a magical effect on me, I guess. Must be my allergy to horses." He touched my cheek gently. "You make me laugh."

"Only by accident."

"And I make you laugh."

"Well, sure. A Wiffle bat as a weapon. Are you really allergic to horses?"

"Yes."

"Do you get a stuffy nose?" I asked. "Or hives? Swollen eyes?"

"Josie." He touched my lips with his fingers, shutting me up pretty effectively. "Think about it, okay? I want you, I want you to be mine. My girlfriend. I can't share you with anybody else. It's just how I am. I know there are a lot of guys who probably want to go out with you, and maybe it's fine with them to share you. Maybe it's completely unfair of me even to ask you for this. But I want you to choose me. Just me. Promise me you'll think about it?"

I shrugged. Carson pulled my face close to his and we kissed a little more. He has the softest lips.

"Your mom hates me," I murmured.

"Yours loves me," he answered.

We smiled, and he turned the car back on. "Will you

teach me to drive?" I asked him.

"Is that your price?"

"Forget it."

"No, that's fair. Name your price. I told you, I like to get my way."

I watched him shift, and waited for his hand to make its way over to mine. "I don't have a price," I said, after a while.

"I didn't mean . . ."

"I don't want a boyfriend," I said. "I am not looking to be half of something."

"Half?"

"I'm not girlfriend material, Carson. You don't know me very well, so you'll have to take my word on this. Seriously."

"What if you're wrong?" he asked, downshifting. "What if I see you more clearly than you see yourself?" He pulled into my driveway. "Come by my locker before first period. You know where it is?"

"Yes."

"I've been coming to yours every day. Tomorrow come to mine. Okay? I'll be waiting for you."

"Don't wait."

He smiled at me. That killer smile. "Don't make me."

I ran up the steps to my house, and Mom threw open the door before I got to it. "So?"

"I had a banana split," I said, on my way up to my room.

Ten

FRANKIE CARO AND Margo Van Deusen looked jus-
tifiably confused as to why a tenth grader, particularly an
outlier alternative-type tenth grader, would be in their locker
pod. Carson put his arm around me and whispered into my
ear, "I told you I always get what I want."

"Ew," I said, but didn't push him away too hard; it felt so
nice, his mouth in my hair, near my ear.

"Come out to lunch with us," he said, into my mess of
hair. "We're gonna get some pizza. Pick you up outside the
main door?"

"I don't have a pass," I said, pulling back. Enough is
enough, and my legs had to carry me the rest of the day.
Phew.

"So what?" he countered.

"So I'm a sophomore."

"So what?" he repeated with that confidence of a boy who in fact always does get his way. "We'll have fun, I promise."

I shrugged, walking away. "I gotta get to class."

"Pick you up by the front door," Carson called.

I didn't turn back to him; I just kept walking, and almost literally bumped into Michael. "Hey," I said, resisting the urge to look back and see if Carson was watching me. It is not his business!

"Hey yourself," Michael said. "Did you go, yesterday?"

"Yes," I said. "In costume."

"And?"

"They were utterly charmed, I think." I grabbed his arm and turned the corner. Truly it is nobody's business what I do. Truly, truly. "Charmed into catatonia, even."

We hurried down the hall together.

"I haven't finished the lyrics," I apologized.

"Don't bother. I can't get the music right, either. Maybe we'll junk it for now."

"I was planning to work on them last night, but . . ."

"You were studying for the trig test?"

"That's today?" I asked.

Michael just exhaled. He's a grind, despite his stoner appearance. He probably studied all day. Poor guy; he's seriously tightly wound.

"SOHCAHTOA, right?" I asked. "Or Sacagawea? I always get those two confused."

"You'll probably ace it, as usual," he moaned.

"Hey." I stopped in front of him and he crashed into me. "What's up?"

"Nothing."

I gave him a Glasgow kiss, which is not a kiss. It is a rugby move where you smash your forehead into the other guy's nose, breaking it, so you can—I don't know—get the ball or just make the other guy bloody or something. Whatever it is you are trying to do in rugby. I am more into sports vocabulary than sports rules. Or, heaven forbid, playing the things. Ew, all that sweating and exertion. The thought of it made me woozy, right there in the hall. Well, that thought and also having missed Michael's nose and slammed my forehead smack into his hard skull.

"Ouch," he said.

"Wow, that sucked," I said. "Rugby may not be my game after all."

"What?"

"Nothing. Why are you even more depressing than usual today?"

"I'm not," he muttered. "I'm always this depressing."

The trig test wasn't bad, but I glanced over at Michael a couple times during it and he seemed pretty stressed. He collected my work for me one time last year when I had strep throat and found out I usually get 100's on quizzes. I'm not super-gifted like Tru; I'm just a test racehorse. It's just one of those things, like some people don't sink when they go in the pool, some know how to throw a ball so it goes toward the person holding up a mitt. I have no idea how people do those things; I'm good at schoolwork. That works out well because it frees up my time for my hobbies, like lying on the couch eating M&M's.

I went into the cafeteria for lunch, and headed straight to the usual table. There was a time in middle school I used to pretend to be sick during lunch most days, so I could eat in the quiet of the nurse's office, rather than endure the horror of the cafeteria. Hallelujah that high school is so much better than what came before. At least there's a group for me, now. We're the group a new kid with an odd haircut from a foreign country will approach and find sanctuary with. We're the ones who know these are NOT the best years of our lives, these years when we have no rights of self-determination beyond how ridiculous we can make ourselves look.

It's not, in other words, that I had nobody to eat lunch with if I decided not to do as I was told and meet Carson Gold and his Golden friends to go out on the town.

"You're eating with us instead?" Zandra asked. "Are you ill?"

"Thanks a lot," Tru said. "Maybe she likes us better."

"If Carson Gold asked you out to lunch . . ." Zandra asked.

"Oh, I'd go," Tru said, and picked up her book. "No question."

Zandra looked at me, accusingly.

I shrugged. "It's too late now anyway." I unwrapped my

sandwich. "I just, I don't want to make a fool of myself, you know? Jump when he snaps his fingers."

"Like every other girl."

I nodded. "You never want to love somebody more than he loves you."

"Absolutely," Zandra agreed.

"He wants me to be his girlfriend," I whispered.

"What!?" They dragged me to the girls' room and made me tell the whole story, every detail. It was a relief to barf it out.

"So, judging from my reaction at his house and after, don't you think it's better if I just, you know . . ."

"Feign disinterest?" Zandra asked.

"Cultivate disinterest," Tru said.

"Steer clear of him," I suggested. "Maybe I'm allergic to romance."

"Maybe you're just scared," Tru said.

"I'm definitely scared," I said. "Terrified."

"You really like him," Zandra said.

Sadly, slowly, I nodded. They nodded, too, and sat close beside me on the floor of the girls' room until the bell rang.

Carson didn't come by my locker after sixth. Not that I expected him to. But still.

Eleven

ON THE BUS going home, as Michael and I were discussing our plans for his birthday on Sunday, my cell phone rang. I scrambled to get it while dropping my books on Michael and the floor.

"All of them?" I was still asking Michael. "You want to watch the whole trilogy in one day?"

"Definitely," Michael said. "Don't you think? Take ten, twelve hours, including breaks?"

"Sounds good," I agreed, flipping open my phone. "Hello?"

"Missed you at lunch," Carson said.

I felt guilty, suddenly. "I told you I wasn't sure. . . ." Also embarrassed, in front of Michael, who pretended he was reading his book and not eavesdropping. And also, God help me, psyched.

"I was in such a foul mood," Carson said.

"Really?"

"Yeah." He lowered his voice. "I got in a fight."

"You mean an argument? Or like a fistfight?"

Michael looked up. I shook my head, like no, I was wrong, and he dug out his iPod.

"A fistfight," Carson was saying. "With Frankie."

"Really? Are you okay?"

"I'm fine."

"Is he?"

Carson chuckled. "Yeah."

"What were you fighting about?"

"Nothing."

"Tell me."

"No way. I can't."

"Why? Where are you?"

"Locker room. But that's not—I don't want to talk about the fight. I don't care about that anymore. I just wanted to talk to you."

"Okay." Neither of us said anything for a minute.

"I was thinking about you all day," he whispered. "Did you think about me? At all?"

"Yeah," I admitted.

"A little?"

"No," I whispered.

"Good," he whispered. "Did you find it?"

"Find what?"

"Check your pocket."

I shoved my hand into my jacket pocket, and something punctured me. "Ow!"

Michael jumped.

I looked at my hand—my finger was bleeding. He booby-trapped my pocket? "What kind of weirdo are you?" I shrieked into the phone.

"What?" Carson asked, all innocent.

"My finger is bleeding."

Michael looked, concerned. "Gross."

"Your finger is what?" Carson asked.

I tapped the phone against the window. "Do we have a bad connection?"

"No, I just . . ."

"Bleeding," I repeated, articulating. "I am completely not kidding. Actual blood is gushing out of my finger, hemorrhaging all over the bus."

The girl in the seat ahead of us got up on her knees and looked over, to see.

"What happened?" Carson asked.

"Okay, well, maybe not hemorrhaging, but if I squeeze, a full round globule of blood forms there on the tip." I stuck it in my mouth and leaned against the window, dizzy in my lightheaded, blood-lost state. "Did you know I am the one who organized the anti-violence peace rally last year? I am a pacifist, damn it! And now I'm bleeding. What is wrong with you, you sick sicko?"

"What are you talking about?" Carson asked.

"Just because I won't do everything you ask, you do not have to assault me." I hung up.

"Golden Boy?" Michael asked.

I nodded.

"The aggressively normal-looking ones are always the most deeply disturbed," Michael said. "Especially the ones who are always out there tossing a ball around." He gave a little shudder for effect.

"He is a little weird, I think," I agreed. However, I am even more curious than I am hypochondriacal, so I carefully put my hand back into my pocket and pulled out a somewhat crushed rose. Thorn and all. A rose.

"Did he give you that?" Michael asked.

I shrugged as my phone rang again.

"Hi," I managed.

"Don't hang up," Carson said.

I didn't. I just sat there staring at the flower, the first flower a boy has ever given me.

"Assault you?"

"I am bleeding here," I said, squeezing my finger. No blood came out anymore. "Hmm. I may have suffered such significant blood loss there is no more blood in me." He slipped a rose into my pocket? "You gave me a rose."

"Yeah," he said. "I know."

"With a thorn," Michael said, loud.

"I thought I'd dethorned it," he said. "I'm sorry. Who's with you?"

Not going there. "When did you put it in my pocket?"

"You're not the only magician on Earth."

Michael made a big show of picking up his book again. I sunk down, toward the window of the bus, and whispered, "Did you strip it off your mother's rose bushes this morning?"

"No," Carson said indignantly. "It's January; they're not in bloom. How did you know they were rose bushes?"

"You bought it?" I asked. Whoa. He went out and bought me a rose?

"No way," Michael mumbled, without lifting his gaze from the page. I knocked my shoulder into his.

"No," Carson said sheepishly. "It was my sister's birthday, and she was home for the weekend so my dad bought her this arrangement, but she went back to school and . . ."

"You gave me a stolen flower?"

Michael snorted.

"Tacky, huh?" Carson asked. "You're right, I guess. Sorry."

"No," I said. "I love it."

"You do?"

The bus pulled up to our stop. Michael and I quickly gathered our stuff and I followed him down the bus aisle and down the steps, saying, "That's not, I mean, that's funny. A stolen flower. Nobody ever gave me a flower before, and this one's stolen, which is just . . . I mean, thanks. Really."

"Come to the movies with me Saturday night."

"Um . . ."

"I'm paying. Come on," he said. "It's one night out of your life. How bad could it be?"

"Okay," I said. I shrugged at Michael, who was standing there waiting for me to hang up or at least start walking toward home.

"Good," Carson said. I heard something slam in the background. "So? Now that we're going on a date, anyway, will you go out with me?"

"Are you coming to walk the dogs with me?" Michael asked.

"No."

Michael grimaced and left me there, by the side of the road.

"No?" Carson asked.

"I wasn't talking to you."

"Good," Carson whispered. "Say yes to me."

"Carson, why? Why are you doing this? I don't get it. I'm like the one girl in the whole school who doesn't want to go out with you. I'm perfectly happy just to hook up from time to time."

"What do I have to do, Josie?"

"Nothing," I whispered. "That's the point. Nothing."

"We have fun together, right?"

"Yeah, sure," I said. "There are explosions when we kiss. Literally." Carson didn't say anything. I thought maybe my phone died or he hung up or had no idea what I was talking about, so I clarified: "I meant, when I burned up the eggs.

Carson? You there? I wasn't being metaphorical."

"I got it," he said.

I started walking toward home. Ahead of me, Michael was coming out of Annabel and Tom's door with Fluffy and Sarge.

I closed my eyes. "So why mess with a good thing?"

"Because it could be a great thing."

Michael passed me without a smile or a look, heading down to the footbridge with the dogs. "See you Sunday," he mumbled. "Come before ten. Brunch."

I nodded and smiled, but he was already past. I buried my nose in the rose Carson had given me, and imagined what it might feel like to walk around school with Carson the way Emelina Lee had last year, his arm across her shoulders, tucked securely under his wing. His girlfriend. His. No, I don't want to be anybody's. I pictured him looking at me the way he used to look at her, looking at me like he wanted to drink me up, like nobody else existed, like he was going to swallow me whole.

"Josie?"

"Still here," I said into the phone.

"You know what we were fighting about?" Carson asked. "Me and Frankie? You."

"Me?"

"That's all I'm saying."

"What did he say about me?" Now I was mad, though once again the chivalry thing was alarmingly appealing.

"Nothing," Carson said. "He was just teasing me, how whipped I am, over you, and I . . . forget it."

"What?"

"The thing is, he's right. Frankie. I'm whipped. I think about you constantly. Go out with me, Josie. Be my girl-friend. Say yes. For once, say yes."

"Sing for me," I said. I don't know what possessed me.

"Josie," he groaned. "I can't."

I didn't say anything.

"I'm in the locker room."

I grinned, picturing him sitting there on the bench, whispering this conversation into his cell phone. In the background I heard deep boy-voices grunting.

"Coming," he said. "One sec," and then quieter, to me, whispered, "Josie?"

"Yeah," I whispered back. It felt a lot more intimate than our unbuttoned afternoons.

And then I heard this very soft, slightly squeaky voice, completely out of tune, singing, "The farmer in the dell, the farmer in the dell, hi-ho the derry-o . . ."

"Yes," I said, and hung up.

Twelve

SATURDAY NIGHT AND there I was like a girl, staring at myself in the mirror as I tried different things with my hair. Zandra was sleeping over at Tru's and they were watching the first season of *Gilmore Girls* on DVD instead of crashing a party. They were going to keep Tru's cell phone with them in case I had to call them mid-date, for reasons good or bad. Some girl friendships get all strained when one of the girls gets a boyfriend, but as in most things, we are not typical. My friends were happy for me. Tru said I glowed; Zandra lent me an ankle bracelet for luck.

I was about to go to my room and put on my jeans but decided I should weigh myself first. Maybe I had lost some weight, which would boost my confidence. I went to my parents' bathroom to use Mom's scale; my fingers in my belly button the way the pediatrician makes me do it every year at my checkup, I watched the numbers tick up, up, up. I dropped the heavy towel and tried again.

A knock.

I grabbed my towel and wrapped it around me. "What?"

"What are you doing?" my father asked, coming into the bathroom holding the newspaper, which could only mean one thing.

"Weighing the possibilities," I answered.

"In my bathroom?"

I kicked the scale under the vanity, then pulled all the hair off my face with my two hands. "Does my face show too much like this?"

My father looked at me briefly. "I'm not sure what that question means," he said.

I whipped a ponytail holder around the hair and stared at him. "What do you think? Better like this?" I pulled the ponytail holder out. "Or like this?"

"Um," he said. "I may not be qualified to say, Josie. Did you ask you mother?"

I grunted at him. "You are just taking up space here, Dad."

"I know," he said. "I made some dinner. Manicotti. Don't tell Mom. You know, the dairy thing."

"I'm not even lactose intolerant."

"I know. She just . . . she worries about you."

I pushed past him. "Do you think I need more eyeliner?" I asked on my way out of their room.

"No," he said. "You're beautiful without all that goop. Did you try the new shoes?"

I went to my room, pulled on my jeans and two long-sleeve T-shirts. A belt? No. Back to my own bathroom for more eyeliner. I was mentally saying all kinds of nasty stuff about my father, and my mother, too, who was at an event celebrating a drug that supposedly makes you fart less, her biggest account, and therefore not home to help her daughter get ready for her first real date like a good mother should—though even as I thought this I knew the last thing I actually wanted was my mother to be home, critiquing me at that point; at least my father thinks I'm beautiful, at least he says he does. I smudged on some lip gloss and immediately smeared it right off with some toilet paper. The truth is, for once it was not my mother's fault, or my father's. I was a wreck all on my own steam.

Breathe, Josie. Just breathe. I'm not magically half of something; I'm still whole, wholly myself, just myself going on a date.

A date? Who goes on a date, is the thing? Maybe Grandma in the 1950s, in a poodle skirt. But me? There has obviously been a mistake. Something has been done wrong. Or something wrong has been done.

What?

Carson Gold, the gorgeous captain of the lacrosse team, starter on the basketball team, president of the senior class, accepted-early-at-Harvard boy, was about to pick me up in his cute white sports car, along with his hot best friend and his hot best friend's gorgeous girlfriend, and we were all going to go see a movie. How was I supposed to concentrate on a movie? I love movies. But still, there was such a severe element of unreality in the circumstances that I was having trouble accepting the fact that this part wasn't the movie I was watching, while crunching popcorn next to Michael and rolling our eyes at how unrealistic movies always are about teenagers: There is no way that odd, independent Josie Dondorff, who never found the smooth or stereotypical way through any part of life, totally non-cheerleader-beach-blanket-white-bread Josephine Dondorff, would end up as Carson Gold's girlfriend. Even the word seemed like something from a few generations ago. Girlfriend?

Zandra and Tru kept shrieking all that afternoon: Carson Gold's girlfriend!

And yet it was happening. Yes. I'm his girlfriend, I whispered to myself in the mirror. I am a songwriter, a clown, a friend, a klutz, a chocoholic, *and* a girlfriend. I shook my head at the giddy grin on my too-round, too-flat face. My jumble of hair still hid me somewhat but even down it couldn't completely obliterate how dementedly happy I looked.

Where was my scowl?

I tried, failed, and finally gave myself a second just to smile at my own reflection. I like him. He likes me. He chose me, out of everybody; he looked around our whole high school and chose me. And I chose him right back. Well, of course. Why shouldn't I? Anybody would choose him. He is smart, fun, funny, cute, and sweet.

Just like me! I am all those things, too. Absolutely. Just because not everybody has noticed all that about me does not mean it's not true: I am smart, funny, fun, cute, and sweet. I am the catch of all catches. If I weren't me I might want to go out with me, too. I may be falling in love with my own self!

I tried a ponytail again. Really? He likes how that looks? He can't possibly. It is just such a large face. I let my hair down again and shook it out around my face, pressed my hands against my thighs. Are they too big?

Youch! Whose thoughts are these? Not mine. Some boring girl somewhere must have been shocked to find herself thinking about whether there is such a thing as objective morality.

I tried to concentrate on objective morality instead. Are some things just wrong, or does context always matter? Is anything real or is it all an illusion? What if . . .

What if he really likes me?

He likes ME. He has seen my thighs, he has seen my hair. He not only chose me, he pursued me. He sang "The Farmer in the Dell" to me, for goodness' sake. Maybe Carson Gold, ironically, actually *is* someone deep and open-minded, creative and individualistic, and he's just been judged shallow and predictable by all of us because of how beautiful he looks. Maybe he recognized me immediately as his kindred spirit, and he sensed that I am the one who can set that part of him free. Maybe we really are meant for each other. As weird as that would be.

I closed my eyes and buried my nose in the rose Carson had given me, in its little glass vase on my bathroom counter. Mmm. It still smelled rosy, despite turning slightly black at the petals' edges. My rose.

The doorbell rang. Dad said, "I'll get it!"

"No!" I almost tripped over the orthotic shoes my father had left outside the bathroom door for me to wear, running to answer it. Sorry, Dad. Not wearing old lady shoes on my first high school date; too bad. I stomped into my black work boots and whipped open the door for my boyfriend.

Thirteen

FRANKIE AND MARGO were in the backseat. I sat up front, next to Carson. He leaned over and kissed me on the lips before he turned the car on.

On the way to the movies, I sang along with the radio, but quieter than when it's just me and Carson. Margo leaned forward and said something to Carson, something that sounded like "Remember the nuts?" He nodded and smiled, and in the back Frankie started laughing. Since I had no idea what that meant I just kept singing, a little softer. I couldn't help wondering how many inside jokes there were going to be that I could not possibly understand, as the new girl, and also how many other girls Frankie and Margo have met tucked under Carson's big arm. It made me feel anonymous and peculiar at the same time.

Frankie pulled Margo back toward him and they started

making out. I know because I turned around to smile gamely, to show I wasn't intimidated by her obnoxious assertion of prior knowledge. His hand was touching her cheek as he kissed her mouth, and her hand was against his jacket. Her long reddish-brown hair was tucked behind her ear, which had a small gold hoop in it. No makeup, but then she didn't need any; she was just naturally beautiful. So was Frankie, in a different way: he was about the same height as Margo, shorter than Carson, and his black hair curled up where it hit his collar. His eyes were so dark you couldn't see the pupils. Maybe it's because I was still wondering what he had said about me to Carson, but I felt like there was something a little subversive about him, a little more dark and risky than either Carson or Margo, who were both bright sunlight.

And me? How did I fit into this scene? I took a pen out of my back pocket and wrote OK on the palm of my hand, to remind myself that I was fine, low stress, this was just a night among thousands in my life; if it sucked completely, I'd have a funny story to tell Michael tomorrow for his birthday, during a bathroom break.

We pulled into the parking lot down the hill from the movie theater. I turned around again and said to the kissing couple, "So! You psyched for the movie? Who wants popcorn?"

They pulled their mouths out of each other's and looked at me. Carson yanked up the emergency brake. "I do," he said. When we all got out of the car, he threw his arm across my shoulder. I fit perfectly. It felt good in there. We walked up the hill ahead of Margo and Frankie.

"Your money's no good here," Carson told me, pushing my wallet away and paying for my movie ticket himself.

"Let's go get popcorn," Margo suggested to me.

I followed her over there.

"Larges?" she asked.

"Extra larges," I said and, to my surprise, she grinned.

"Yeah." She turned to the guy behind the counter. "Two extra larges."

"Two?" he asked her. "You sure? They're very big."

"We're big women," Margo said.

When he passed the two huge, overflowing buckets across the counter, I asked him, "Don't you have anything bigger than this?"

Margo cracked up. I liked her completely. I felt myself begin to relax. We paid for our troughs of popcorn and turned around. "Uh-oh," Margo said.

"What?"

She pointed with her chin. "Emelina Lee." I looked across toward the front door. There she was, Carson's famous ex-girlfriend, in all her glory, crossing the red-carpeted lobby hand in hand with a gorgeous, slightly older-looking guy, who was sophisticatedly wearing a gray flannel scarf and a coat instead of a ski jacket. Emelina's long black hair was back in a French braid, which just made her high cheekbones look that much more stunning. People stopped their conversations as she passed. She was wearing a black turtleneck, black pants, black high-heeled boots, and a red leather jacket.

Margo sighed.

"She sure has good posture," I pointed out.

Turning to smile at me, Margo said, "Yes. Perfect."

"Matches the rest of her," I added.

"Meow," Margo whispered.

My mouth dropped open to protest, but what could I say? She was right, I needed a saucer of milk to go with my attitude.

Margo smiled at Emelina, who had stopped right in front of us. "Hi, Emelina."

"Hi, Margo," Emelina said. "How are you?"

"Great," Margo said. "You playing first singles again?"

"Yeah," Emelina said. "Getting psyched. We should be good this year. This is Daniel. He's in for the weekend."

"Hi, Daniel," Margo said.

"Margo is on the tennis team with me," Emelina explained to Daniel. "She's a junior."

"Ah," said Daniel. "Tough year."

Margo smiled and nodded.

Carson and Frankie had made their way over and Emelina introduced Daniel to them. He and Carson gripped each other's hands super hard, like they were trying to see who could crush whose bones.

To break the tension, and maybe also to remind myself

that I hadn't gone home yet, despite nobody's seeming to have noticed, I said, "I'm Josie."

They all turned to look at me, considering this news. Emelina held out her hand and said, "Hi, Josie."

I took her hand and squished hard, jumping to the offensive since I figured if she was a star tennis player she could take me on pure strength. She gave me a small pulse of a squeeze and let go. When it took me a second to realize we were done with that, she raised one arched eyebrow at me.

"You look familiar," Emelina said, retrieving her hand. "You don't go to school with us, do you?"

"Yup," I said. "Sure do. But I don't play tennis. I wanted to, but then I heard a rumor that there's some running around and sweating involved, so . . ."

Emelina smiled slightly, acknowledging her understanding that I was kidding around, although in fact I wasn't. I spread my feet a little farther apart, imitating Carson's squared-off stance. If Emelina and Daniel challenged us to a fistfight, all I can say is it's a good thing Carson is strong. But I didn't want to let down our side ahead of time by hiding behind Carson. Well, I did, actually, but I resisted. A few popcorns tumbled out of my vat, onto the floor. Emelina and Dan I guess didn't want any popcorn.

"Hmm," Emelina said, looking down at the mess I had made. "Anyway, we should get seats . . ."

Everybody nodded at that, but nobody budged.

"This is fun, huh?" I said. I shoved a handful of popcorn

into my mouth and started to chew, loudly.

Carson, evidently remembering who his date was, took two steps toward me, and slung his arm protectively across my shoulders. Emelina's face changed only slightly, briefly, and then she smiled at Carson.

"Hey," Carson said. "You guys want to come over tomorrow for the Eagles game?"

Emelina glanced up at Daniel. "Carson is famous for his Eagles parties."

"You want to go?" Daniel asked her.

Emelina waited a second, then another, before answering. "Sure," she said. "It's been awhile."

"We'll be there, then," Daniel said. "What can we bring?"

"Nothing," said Carson, squeezing my shoulders. "We'll see you there."

Emelina blinked her eyes twice at Carson, then started toward the door of the movie. We all watched her go. I felt Carson deflate a little.

"Who was that?" Frankie asked. "Daniel?"

"He's a sophomore at Princeton," Carson answered, looking at the space Emelina had been in. "She met him that weekend she went up in the fall, after she got in early."

"Oh," said Frankie. "That's him?"

"Yeah," Margo whispered, grabbing his hand. "Let's sit at the back. Come on."

As we followed Margo and Frankie in, I asked Carson, "You okay?"

"Fine," he said, and stopped. He yanked me toward him and kissed me hard on my mouth. I was a little squashed so I tried to pull back a bit, but he was holding me tight. When he finally let go, I looked up at him. He pushed my hair away from my face and tucked it behind my ear. "You're beautiful."

He was staring at me, with that devouring look in his eyes.

"No," I whispered. "You're thinking of . . ."

"Of you." He kissed me lightly, then again. "Only you."

Fourteen

THE MOVIE WAS awful, not just because it was disgustingly violent but also because, except for Carson holding my hand, absolutely nothing interesting happened. Not that I was paying so much attention to the plot or anything other than Carson's warm fingers interlaced with mine, but other people were actually groaning out loud. Next to us, Frankie and Margo were the only ones who didn't seem to notice. Maybe because their eyes were closed the whole time.

"You want to go back to Frankie's after?" Carson whispered to me, while the idiots on screen were running away from yet another fireball, machine guns in hand. "His parents are away."

I shrugged. I am just as happy to mess around as the next person, with the possible exception of Frankie and Margo, because, my goodness. And I thought I was a nympho.

"We don't have to," Carson said. "If you don't want to."

"Okay," I said.

He kissed the hair right over my ear. I so love that. It made my skin tingle, all the way down to my knees. "Okay yes or okay no?"

At the end of the movie, we headed out to the car. Margo said she had to go to the bathroom and asked if I wanted to come. I said no thanks, and stood around in the lobby with Frankie and Carson.

Emelina and Daniel emerged from the movie theater holding hands, blinking, and glided toward us.

"So . . ." Carson said.

"So," echoed Emelina.

"That was a piece of crap, huh?" I said.

Everyone smiled. Daniel said, "You think so?"

"You didn't?" I asked.

"I don't know," Daniel said. "I guess I thought it was a brilliant failure. It tried to turn all the Hollywood tropes on their heads, which I appreciate, but ultimately didn't come to any kind of, you know . . ."

"Satisfying conclusion," Emelina finished, for him.

Carson nodded slowly. "That's what it needed," he agreed.

"And maybe a satisfying beginning," I suggested. "And I bet a satisfying middle would've helped, too."

"You're a junior?" Daniel asked me.

"Sophomore," I admitted.

"Ah," he said.

"See you tomorrow?" Emelina asked me, and without waiting for an answer, she and Daniel swept out toward the doors. Again heads turned as they left. Maybe it was their walk.

"What happened?" Margo asked, approaching us.

"Nothing," Carson said. "Let's go."

It was starting to snow when we got outside, so I pulled my hood up. Carson let the car heat up for a minute.

"You coming over?" Frankie asked.

"I don't think so," Carson answered. "We're gonna, um . . ."

"You know my parents aren't . . ."

"He said no, Frankie," Margo said. "Shh."

I sat back in my seat and stared out the window. I didn't want to be a baby, or a killjoy. Maybe I just don't know how to be cool. I sank down in my seat. Carson turned on the radio but this time I didn't sing at all. We drove to the south end quietly. Carson pulled up in front of a small white house with a chain-link fence in front.

"Home sweet home," Frankie said.

"Can you let them out?" Carson asked me.

I got out quickly and released the seat so Frankie and Margo could uncurl from the back. They both ducked down to say bye to Carson, then turned and walked up the dark path to the front door. Carson peeled out while I was closing the car door.

"Are you mad?" I asked.

"No," he said.

We rode in silence for a while.

"What are you thinking about?"

"Nothing," he said.

"Nothing?" I asked. "Nothing? Really? Wow, that's so Zen of you. Maybe it comes with your magic witch-eye. You really have a totally empty mind? That's like the highest level of karmic enlightenment, isn't it?"

"Do you ever stop talking?" he asked.

I didn't say anything for a minute. "Sorry," I came up with. Ah, well. It was lovely while it lasted.

Carson turned down a narrow winding road with no houses as far as you could see, and pulled over onto the frozen grass.

"So," I felt myself start defensively chattering, powerless to shut up. "Do you think Daniel was right about the movie having some meta-meaning, like that it was trying to be a movie about an action movie? Because if so, I totally missed that. Or do you think Daniel is just full of—"

Carson interrupted by leaning across the gearshift and planting his mouth full on mine. We made out for a few minutes. When he pulled back a little, I finished my (edited) thought: "Himself."

Carson took off his jacket and kissed me some more.

"Do I talk too much?" I asked him.

"Yes. Shh." He kissed me some more.

"Mostly when I'm nervous," I said, into the inside of his

mouth.

He unzipped my jacket and slowly untucked my shirts, but didn't stick his hand inside. "What time are you coming over tomorrow?" he murmured, pushing my jacket down off my arms.

"I can't," I said. Michael's birthday. The entire Lord of the Rings, uncut, all day and night. "Sorry."

"Yes, you can," Carson said. He kissed little kisses up the side of my neck, which made me all tingly again. By the time he got to my ear I was practically panting. I moved my mouth to his and we made out awhile longer. He unhooked my bra through my shirts, on his first try.

As he slipped his hand toward my waist, I said, "You still like her, don't you?"

"Who?" he asked, kissing me with tender little teasing kisses.

"Emelina."

He pulled back and stared at me. "Why would you say that?"

"I saw the way you looked at her."

He gripped his jaw closed. "I can't believe you would say that." He looked angrily out the window, at the darkness.

My fingers felt a little shaky. I didn't trust myself to say anything so I just very slightly shrugged. My unhooked bra was making my T-shirts all lumpy. I crossed my arms over my misshapen self.

"Why would I have broken up with her, if I still liked

her? Why would I be here with you, if I still liked her?" He kept his face turned away from me.

"I thought," I began, but didn't finish, because you cannot say to somebody, Oh, I thought she dumped YOU. Even if it's true.

He looked at me, shooting daggers. "You thought what?"

No way. Not going there. I may be only a sophomore but I am not that dumb.

"You thought so little of yourself that you can't imagine I would want you, rather than Emelina?"

I opened my mouth to protest that but the calamitous truth of his statement stopped me, put a cork right in my throat, as surely as if I had swallowed it. I could feel it lodged there, in fact.

"Oh, Josie," he said, softening. Ah, the way he looked at me. It was back. *Thank you, thank you God.*

"I . . ." *Don't mess up again, Josie, just shut the hell up.*

He touched my cheek softly with his big hand. "Josie."

A tear fell from my eye onto his finger.

"How can I convince you how amazing you are?"

"No," I said.

"Yes! You have this amazing body. . . ."

I shook my head. Body? My butt is too big, my boobs are too small . . . and Emelina? She's perfect, skinny and long-legged and fashionable, with her long silky black hair, perfect skin, red lips. . . . Nobody in the world would say that I am pretty next to her.

" . . . and a gorgeous face, for those of us lucky enough to get a glimpse, and you are so smart and independent and sharp and oh, Josie, why would you be jealous of anybody?"

A few more tears fell. My whole body was shaking.

"I'm fat," I whispered.

"You are NOT fat. You are perfect. Oh, please don't turn into every other girl. You are the only girl I know who isn't constantly weighing herself."

I swallowed. The last thing I needed was bulbous-red-from-crying nose. I managed a smile, a weak smile. "Sorry," I whispered.

He wiped the last tear off my cheek with his thumb. "You are perfect. Perfect for me."

"Right back at you."

That made him smile. "Meant for each other, right?"

"Right." I was still shaking a little. "Yes."

He leaned toward me again, his lips soft and warm. "Tomorrow," he whispered, "come a little early and maybe we can sneak up to my room . . ."

"Is it really important," I asked, hating myself. "I mean, to you, for me to come, because I have . . ."

"I want to show you off," he said simply. "Is that so bad? You're my girlfriend. I want to hold your hand while we watch the Eagles kill the Cowboys and at the same time watch every other guy get jealous, because you are sitting on the couch next to *me*."

"Seriously?"

"Josie, it's been over for a long time with Emelina. She and I are just trying to be friends again."

"Why?"

"Why? Why are you friends with your friends? We like each other, we care about each other, we went through a lot together."

"Yeah, but . . ."

"Friends. You have to trust me. Don't you trust me?"

"I guess," I said.

"I trust you not to be chasing Michael Addison around anymore."

"I was never chasing Michael around."

"You know what I mean," Carson said. "Why don't you want to come over? These parties are important to me, and you know it's the NFC championship this week. You knew that, right?"

I didn't want to lie so I said, "Who doesn't?"

"True," he answered, satisfied. "So come."

"I . . ."

"Why can't you just say yes to me for once?"

I have plans with Michael, was the true answer, but how could I say so, then?

"Let me think about it," I said.

"One of these days you're going to wear out my patience, gorgeous," Carson scolded, and leaned over to place his soft lips on mine again. "Mmm," he said, tasting me. "Oh, Josie." Again we got into making out. He is an amazing kisser, and his hands, oh, man, his hands. They were exploring me, my arms, my hands, my hair, my earrings, each of which he kissed, lightly, before making his way back to my mouth. He pulled back only very slightly, so I could feel his words with my own lips. "Wear a ponytail, okay?" he asked, and kissed me again. "You know that makes me so crazy. Or a braid," he suggested. "I would love to see you in a braid. Mmm."

Fifteen

"WHY IS YOUR hair like that?" Michael asked, when I got to his house at nine thirty.

"Thanks," I said. "Happy birthday." I handed him the box I had brought.

"Hi, Josie," his mom said, from the kitchen. "You're really going to sit here watching these dumb movies with Michael for twelve hours?"

"Ten," Michael corrected her. He shrugged at me. "Okay, twelve with breaks. You two always gang up on me."

His mother winked at me and I wished for the house to collapse and swallow us all up instantly. I turned away from him and gestured toward the little gift I had brought. "Aren't you going to open it?"

"Soon," Michael said. He likes anticipation, too. "Let's eat."

We went into the kitchen, where his mom had laid out a great spread, as always: homemade corn muffins, two bowls of berries, and a frittata, fresh out of the oven. "You are wonder-woman," I told her gratefully, taking my seat at her table.

"You know it," she said, then added sheepishly, "but unfortunately I got called in to work. I should've gotten someone else to take the call for me. I can't believe this woman went into labor. . . ."

"Stop apologizing, Mom," Michael groaned.

"I just feel bad. It's your birthday, and now Dad and I both have to work. . . ." His dad is great, too, very sincere; he works really hard and supposedly he's this incredibly powerful lawyer, but his voice is slow and soft. He noticed when I cut my own hair last fall and complimented me on it. I love the whole family.

Michael shook his head. "We're going to be in front of the TV when you get home, just like when you leave," he said. "Seriously, don't worry, okay?"

I smiled weakly up at her. She breathed deep and kissed Michael on his hair. "Sixteen," she murmured. "What a fine young man you are, son." She turned away quickly and scrubbed a pan in the sink. Michael rolled his eyes for my benefit but we knew each other too well; I could see everything going on in there, how much he wants to make his mom (as well as his dad) proud, how close they all are, how much he loved the compliment she just gave him, and even probably how disappointed he was that they had to work on his birthday. He is a fine young man, though; he would never be a pouty brat about their needing to work like I'd be to my parents. Boy was I hating myself at that moment, especially because I couldn't help glancing down at my watch.

Michael's mom turned around and watched us chowing down for a minute, then said, "Josie, you look different."

"Ponytail."

"Yes, but not just that. You look, sort of, scrubbed."

I could feel myself blushing. Yes, I had scrubbed myself pretty well, used a big handful of my mom's expensive facial scrub and did my eyeliner more like Emelina's, subtle and slightly smudgy, no eye shadow. I felt very exposed suddenly, with no hair to hide behind.

Michael glanced up to check, and shrugged. "You look the same to me."

"Thanks."

"Okay," his mom said. "I really should run."

"Bye." Michael wiped his mouth and stood up, bringing his plate to the sink. "Thanks, Mom. Don't worry, it's fine. Come on, Josie. I have all the DVDs in my room."

I carried my plate over, too. "What do you mean, in your room?"

"I'll show you," he said.

"I'm so happy Michael has you," his mom whispered to me. "Bye guys!"

"Deliver a good baby," Michael called back.

I followed him up the stairs. As soon as Michael opened his bedroom door, I saw his new TV. "Wow," I said.

"Yeah," he said. "Too much, huh?" He turned it on and flipped through some special features with his remote, then sat down on his bed. I leaned against his desk and watched him open the wrapping on my gift.

"It's not that great," I apologized. "It's just a little thing."

He threw the wrapping to the side and opened the box. He pulled the keychain out, looking puzzled, until he opened the black leather folded thing hanging off the ring, and saw the pictures of Fluffy and Sarge, one in each mini-frame. I watched his half-smile spread his mouth, then grow bigger.

"It's supposed to be for pictures of your kids, I think," I explained. "Or, like, if you are sweethearts, or maybe if you have two girlfriends, but I thought . . ."

As I babbled, he stood up, walked to his door, shut it, came over to me and leaned right up against me. "I love it," he whispered, and put his arms around me and his mouth onto mine.

I didn't close my eyes. I could feel my body molding to his, by habit, even maybe by desire. *But wait, no, I can't do this.*

I pushed him back, with increasing pressure until he stopped making out with me. "I can't," I whispered.

"She won't come up," he whispered back, pressing back into me.

"No," I said.

Startled, Michael backed up. "What?" He still had the keychain in his hand.

"I can't."

"Can't what?"

"Kiss you," I said.

He backed up a couple more steps. "Why not?"

I swallowed, turned around, ran my hand over his neat desk set. "I'm going out with Carson Gold."

"No," Michael said.

I nodded, too chicken even to face him.

"You can't be."

I shrugged. "I am. And, um, the thing is? I kind of told him I would stop by, for a, like a half hour or so this afternoon, just like, you know, around one, one thirty or so, like an errand, and then I'll come right back."

"No," Michael growled. "No, you're not doing that."

My cell phone rang. Great. Tru.

"Hello?"

"Josie, you never called us last night. What happened?"

"Nothing," I said. Michael was glaring at me, his teeth and fists clenched. "Listen, Tru, can I . . ."

"How far did you go?" Zandra demanded. She had clearly grabbed the phone from Tru and her voice was loud, too loud.

"I'll call you guys later, okay?" I hung up on them. They were going to be really mad, but I had to put out one fire at a time. Michael looked about ready to kill me.

"Michael, I just have to go for a few . . ."

"You're not going!"

"You can't tell me what to do, Michael. I have to go for like a few minutes. Please! What is the big deal? Your parents aren't even going to be here the whole day, and you're not giving them a hard time. Let's just watch the stupid movie!" I pressed the power button of his TV.

He clicked it off, immediately, with the remote, which he chucked hard onto his bed, then grabbed my arm and spun me around. "What about me?" he whispered harshly.

I pulled away, slowly but definitely. "What about you?"

"You're just dumping me? Happy birthday, good-bye?"

"No," I protested. "I'm not dumping you. Don't make such a big thing . . ."

"At least be honest, Josie. You are dumping me for the Golden Boy." He turned his back to me, and kind of melted down to sit on his bed. "Why?"

"Michael . . ."

He flung the keychain I had given him across the room. It missed my head by inches, slammed hard into his closed door and landed on his rug.

I came and sat down beside him. "Why don't we just watch the first movie?"

"No," he said. "Go."

"I don't have to be there until one," I argued. "It's not even eleven."

"Get out of here, Josie. I don't want you here."

"What do you want from me, Michael? Come on, don't be a jerk about this."

"What do I want?" He stood up and kicked his desk chair. "What do I want from you? Are you kidding me? I love you! I have been in love with you since like what, kindergarten? What do I want from you? I want to grow up together, I want to grow old together, I want to lose our virginity together."

We stared at each other.

"You do?" I finally asked.

He turned away.

"You never said . . ."

"I didn't think I needed to," he answered. "Or, anyway, you've always said all that about why do people think they have to couple off, be half a unit instead of wholly themselves, all that. Remember that?"

"Yeah."

"But then Golden Boy comes along with his stolen flower and all of a sudden you just forget everything you believe in your rush to get him, the prize: Yes, yes, I'll commit to you, I'll be your girlfriend. I'll do anything, be anything you want, Golden Boy. I bet he even told you to do your hair like that."

"Stop it, Michael."

"Do you love him? Do you even like him? Or do you just like the idea of him?"

I went and picked up the keychain, and put it down on the bed beside Michael. "I like him," I said.

I went to his door and opened it. It was clear we weren't going to be watching the movie, not for one hour, not for ten. I had to go; I couldn't make him forgive me or pretend we could just go on like normal only without fooling around anymore. Maybe I had tried to convince myself we could go back to just friends, like in elementary school, but I guess even I knew that wasn't realistic. Or fair.

"I'm sorry, Michael." I said. "I do. I like him."

Sixteen

I HEADED BACK to my house, cutting through Annabel
and Tom's yard. I could hear Fluffy and Sarge barking at me
from inside, but I didn't look up. I pressed the garage button
with crossed fingers, and surprisingly enough, got lucky: my
dad's car was gone. Phew—they were out; no explanations
necessary for why I was back so soon. The feeling of relief
lasted about three seconds, at which point it was replaced by
loneliness, abandonment, and despair. I turned and looked
around, 360 degrees: all these lawns, mowed to the proper
standards, islands of snow dotting them decoratively; swing
sets and basketball hoops, welcome mats, winding walks, fake
shutters nailed open, all uniformly inviting—and it could
just as easily have been a ghost town. Okay, maybe that's not
fair; mid-January mornings in Pennsylvania aren't famous for
the glut of lemonade stands. But still, I was the only person

in sight, the only person around, standing in front of my half-empty garage with no parental supervision. What would stop me from taking my mother's keys off the hook inside the door and driving her sedate black sedan away from this little hellish bit of paradise forever?

Well, not knowing how to drive might stop me. Or at least slow me down.

I went inside and sat against the fridge to call Tru and Zandra back.

"Oh." Zandra's voice on Tru's phone. "Found a minute for your friends, Glamour Girl?"

"Sorry," I said. "I was just . . . I was at Michael's."

"You are insatiable!" Zandra shrieked.

"Yeah," I said. I felt so tired.

"We're gonna lie around Tru's room all day doing nothing but eating candy and complaining about how boring our lives are. Want to join us?"

"Yes," I said. "But I can't."

"Oh, right, Tru just reminded me—you're spending the day at Michael's for his birthday."

"No," I said. "I, I kind of, just, broke up with him."

"You what? She broke up with Michael. But you're going out with Carson!"

"Exactly."

"Oh. She told Michael about Carson," I heard her tell Tru, and then she asked me, "How'd he take it?"

"Not well."

"You want us to come over? Tru's father will drive us. Right, Tru? We can be there in ten minutes. Tru! Get . . ."

"No, I'm going over to Carson's."

"Oh," she said, and told Tru. "Okay."

"Miss me, okay?"

"We'll try," Zandra said. "Call us if you need backup."

"I will." I hung up and hauled myself upstairs. It was still too early to go over to Carson's. Right then I was wishing I could blow off both the boys I love—I could be eating candy for breakfast with my friends instead of groaning at myself in front of my mother's mirrored wall units. My favorite black sweater didn't look great and original and cool to me, suddenly, despite the thirteen safety pins holding together the rip I had cut from the neck to the shoulder.

I opened my mother's wall unit door. On top of her sweater pile was a new yellow one, with the tissue paper still folded into it. Cashmere. I pulled my hand away. I don't do pastel. My mother must've told me a hundred times that I need to soften my look and I roll my eyes every time.

I ripped off my sweater and pulled my mother's new yellow cashmere over my head. The tissue paper fluttered toward the floor. The deep V neck exposed a lot more of me than I usually do; I closed the door warily, not sure I was ready to see the mirror.

Well. Okay. Not so bad. I stopped myself from stretching it out with my fists; the cashmere clung to my body, showed my curves. Ew, like Mom. She sure has tits, is probably the first thing people think when they see her. Well, so what? I have tits, too. Maybe Mom was right, that I should stop hiding in my big old clothes.

Before I could change my mind, I dashed downstairs, threw on my jacket, hat, and gloves, and pulled my bike out of its spot. For a severely anti-athletic person, I sure get plenty of use from the old thing. Six more months until I can drive. I kicked the kickstand extra hard. Six more months. I glided down the driveway, not looking at the house of my six-months-older friend who was celebrating his birthday alone.

As I rode, I realized suddenly that I had sort of always subconsciously figured I would lose my virginity to Michael, too, and now maybe everything is different and there won't be any going back. The thought that maybe I won't ever lose my virginity to Michael hit me like a loss in itself. Maybe all this time as I was telling myself I didn't want a boyfriend because no way do I ever want to be half a couple, maybe I already was half a couple.

Oh, no.

But also, okay.

As awful as I felt about hurting Michael and losing him, possibly losing his friendship and love forever, and maybe also the love of his parents who would hate me for hurting him, especially on his sixteenth birthday when they were counting on me to be there for him, I was also in a small, weird way kind of happy. Set free.

I sped up and let the wind rip tears from my eyes. I didn't

really want to spend these next twelve hours of my life watching TV with Michael in Michael's house, eating popcorn and sometimes, during the boring parts of the movies, fooling around with each other in our usual half-distracted way, watching the movie out of the corners of our eyes while we kissed. I had thought that's what I wanted to do, but now that I was sprung, it was clear to me that I actually didn't. At all.

Because what I wanted to do with the next twelve hours was be Carson's girlfriend. I wanted him to hold my hand and grab me if the Eagles managed to get a first down, grab me and yell, pull me close and feel Emelina Lee watch me, even as her hand gripped college-boy Daniel's; I wanted to feel her envy shoot across the room to stab me as she remembered what it was like to be Carson's girlfriend, and wonder who I was, this sophomore who had him so smitten, so in love.

In love. I wanted to feel him fall in love with me. I wanted to fall in love with him. I wanted to say whatever was on my mind and watch him smile; feel him look deep into my eyes and shake his head at the wonder of me, at how shocking the intensity of his feelings for me had become, so fast. I wanted him to look at me like he was just barely managing to stop himself from devouring me, and then I wanted him to take me into some back room on a pretext of finding the pickles, and grab me, kiss me hard and deep, and say *Oh man, Josie, oh, what you do to me. I have never felt this way about any other girl before.*

Seventeen

I DROPPED MY bike in Carson's driveway and stumbled up his walk. I rang his doorbell and tightened my ponytail while I waited. Carson opened the door. I smiled, not just at the fact that this time I was not in a clown suit. "Hi," I said to him, leaning forward.

"Hold on," he said. "I mean, come in. Emelina's just telling us the funniest story."

"Great," I said, a master of enthusiasm.

"Well, I'm fine," Emelina was telling the small, actively attractive group. "Unfortunately I can't say the same for the truck."

"The truck?" Carson asked her. "Wait. What happened?"

"Tell them," Daniel urged, and turned to us. "It's a great story." He gave Emelina's hand a squeeze. I took off my gloves in case anybody developed the urge to squeeze mine.

Emelina leaned against the door frame. "You remember my grandparents' old ugly orange couch, up at the mountain house?" she asked Carson, who nodded. "Well, it finally collapsed. My parents had just ordered new leather furniture, so my grandparents said they would love to have our old things. It was just a matter of getting the furniture to them. Well, I would do anything for Gingy and Pops, you know them, Carson. Aren't they great?"

"Great." Carson nodded. "Absolutely."

"Everybody loves them. My parents said it's not worth it, we'll buy them new furniture—but I love that old stuff. I have a hard time saying good-bye, I guess. . . ." She smiled a little. "So I said rent me a truck and I'll haul the furniture up to the mountain house myself."

"Your parents let you?" I asked, interrupting.

She looked at me, confused, and shrugged. "What were they going to say?"

I was starting to sweat so I unzipped my jacket. Also I wanted Carson to see my tight sweater. "My parents have a lot to say about what I eat for lunch," I answered, taking the jacket off, slowly. Carson noticed. Good.

"And you listen?" Emelina was asking me, meanwhile.

"No," I said. "But I think if I asked them to rent me a truck, they'd . . . hesitate."

Emelina shrugged. "Not mine."

"Go on," Carson said, turning back to her. "So you rented the truck . . ."

"I rented the truck," she said. "I brought it home and, with some help, loaded the old furniture into the truck and kissed my parents good-bye."

Daniel gave a little stifled laugh, either about kissing her parents good-bye or in anticipation of what was to come, I don't know. I didn't really care. I was busy scouting out a place to put down my coat, here at the Emelina show.

Yes, I know. Meow.

"I started down the street. I could hear the stuff clattering around a little in the back, but it sounded okay. I had never driven a truck before. I love to drive, you know I do."

Carson nodded. I suppressed a gag.

"But normally I drive my little—you know my car."

He smiled at her. Bitch.

I squeezed Carson's arm and whispered, "Where's the bathroom?"

He pointed, without taking his eyes off Emelina. I slunk off to the bathroom and left my stuff in a small pile outside it.

As I washed my hands, I considered calling Zandra and Tru. I didn't want people to hear me and think I was talking to myself in there, though, so I dried my hands on the towel and came out. I would tell them about Emelina later and we'd be merciless about her.

More people had arrived, and Emelina was still talking: "It was completely stuck in the underpass! So I threw it into reverse, floored it, and flew out backwards."

Every mouth (except mine) dropped open. Every eye was riveted to her beautiful face. I considered throwing up, as a diversion.

"I climbed down from the truck," she continued, softer, so everybody had to lean forward. "All the people were very nice. They got out of their cars to see if I was okay, which of course I was, and the truck looked fine too, not at all scraped on the sides, of course, which is where I was looking, but then I noticed all the wheels were resting on a huge piece of metal. I didn't remember driving over a big sheet of metal on the way in so I asked, 'What is that under my truck?' "

"And what was it?" I asked. My voice boomed. It sounded strangely impatient. Go figure.

"The roof," Emelina smoothly answered. "The roof of the truck had popped off and I had driven onto the top of it. So I had to back up some more to get off it, and some of the guys helped me pull it over to the side of the road. They were so wonderful, all the people there, helping me, all of them, out of their cars, and it was cold, starting to snow. Remember? Just before Christmas. The first snow."

Well, well, I thought. *How* It's a Wonderful Life.

"So then what happened?" Carson prompted.

"Nothing, really," Emelina said. "That was that. I thanked all the people, who were all clapping and cheering. It was quite the party by then. Funny." She chuckled to herself.

Oh, yes, I thought. *What a riot!*

"Some of them were beeping and chanting my name as I made a U-turn. What a scene. I waved good-bye and took the long way around to the highway, and brought the stuff to my grandparents' house."

"You brought it?" I had to ask. "You drove the four hours without the roof?"

"And back," she answered. "The next day."

"In the snow?" I smiled at her. Or bared my teeth, anyway.

"Topless!" Emelina said. "So to speak."

She came right over to me, laid her long fingers on my sleeve, and asked me quietly, intimately, "But do you want to hear the funniest part?"

Not really.

"You have to hear this," Daniel said.

"That wasn't the funniest part?" I asked.

"No," Emelina leaned against the banister, right beside Carson. "When I returned the truck, sans lid, they asked if there were any problems with the rental. I said no, not at all, only the top popped off down at the underpass on Chesterton, and it was there on the side, in the bushes. The guy wrote it down and said, 'Thank you for renting with U-Haul.'"

Carson laughed. "He said thank you for . . . ?"

"I kid you not." Emelina held up her right hand, like she was taking an oath. "So yesterday morning I got something from U-Haul in the mail, and I figured, here it is. They're suing me, they want a payment, something. I opened the letter and what was it?"

We didn't know. We all waited.

"A check for fifty dollars!"

Nobody moved. "I don't get it," I finally said.

"My deposit, I guess. Good gig, huh? If they need tops popped off any more trucks, I could get rich. My dad's theory is that it happens all the time. Anyway, now the mountain house is full of the furniture I love, so all it needs is the people I love—the weekend after next. Carson, come. And bring—" She gestured toward me.

I had to stop myself from saying I would rather yank off all my fingernails than spend the weekend hearing more of your never-ending, self-aggrandizing, stupid stories. But Carson had finally turned toward me, so I stifled my growl and imitated a smile.

"We'll go cross-country skiing, snowmobiling, build a fire, it'll be great. You'll love Gingy and Pops, Joey, everybody does."

"Josie," I corrected. Grrr.

"Right. We'll ask Margo and Frankie, too, if you want. Sound good?"

"As long as you're not driving," Carson told her.

She smacked him on his head and stood up. We all followed her into the family room. Like a happy little parade.

Eighteen

I HAD NO idea what was happening in the game. When other people jumped up, I jumped up, too; when they groaned, I joined in. I had no mind of my own, or what little I had was used up on sensation: Carson's palm against mine, the smell of his hair as he lowered his head toward my face, the pressure and heat of his leg thrown over my own.

At halftime we all went out in the backyard to toss a ball around. Carson split us up onto teams, choosing me first. First time in my life that ever happened. I whispered to him, "I suck at football."

"I figured," he whispered back. "Go deep."

With only a vague idea what that meant, I ran around like a lunatic, waving my hands in the air but praying he wouldn't throw the ball my way. He didn't. Emelina caught a perfect spiral from Daniel on the other team and scored. I cheered for them. What did I care? She could win any football game in the world; I was Carson's girlfriend and she wasn't.

Carson grabbed me. "What are you doing, you dope? They're on the other team!"

"Haven't you ever heard of good sportsmanship?" Emelina said, defending me, I guess.

Carson let go of me and said to her, "I'll show you good sportsmanship."

"Promises, promises," she answered, and walked away.

I watched her go. Carson grabbed me from behind again but I pulled away. "Hey," he said. I shrugged him off. He grabbed my hand and tugged me around to his side yard. "Somebody's jealous," Carson said, unzipping my jacket. "That turns me on." He slipped his hands inside and ran his hands down my shoulders, across my chest, up my sides. I felt like clay he was sculpting, felt every contour of myself get molded by his hands. When his mouth came down to mine, there was no resistance left in my lips. I felt his fingers touch my neck, my earlobes, my earrings.

"Everything about you turns me on," Carson whispered. "Your great-grandmother's earrings, even. Is that weird?"

"Yes," I whispered back.

He groaned. "Mmm, how you never take them off—it makes me want to get you completely naked. . . ."

"Carson . . ."

"Someday?" he asked. "Someday, not now, obviously, but

someday, will you take them off, for me? Be completely naked with me. Come to Emelina's, in the mountains. Oh, wouldn't that be so great?" He kissed my neck, his hands slipping under my sweater. My mother's sweater.

"I don't know," I said. I could feel the cold air hitting the strip of bare skin he was exposing.

"Just imagining you taking off everything, even your earrings . . ."

"I never take them off."

"I know," he said, touching my earrings and kissing me again. "Promise me, though, someday. Josie, please. Say maybe, at least."

"Maybe, at least," I said.

"Second half!" his father yelled. "It's starting."

Carson groaned. "I'm gonna explode. Ugh." He held my hand walking back in. I watched Emelina notice that.

We settled back into the same spots. Carson's cheeks were pink and he smelled like winter. I tried to watch the game instead of just him. It was a challenge. After about ten minutes he kind of untangled from me and whispered, "Will you get me a soda?"

"Um, okay," I whispered back.

I stood up and started to make my way across the family room, past and over people. Everybody looked attached to the TV by invisible strings from their eyes to the screens, loose smiles on their faces, slumped in random positions all draped on one another. It was nice, actually. I had always imagined these groupings of beautiful people being high-tension affairs, with secret codes and competitive strife, each person checking out everyone else, jockeying for position and superiority. These guys all seemed relaxed and comfortable, easy. Like normal people only better-looking. I wondered if maybe, possibly, I fit in among them.

I went to the kitchen to get Carson a soda, but stopped when I got to the fridge. It was full of pictures, and beside it was a whole bulletin board filled with more photos as well as lots of invitations, letters, and a calendar. I guess I started reading and lost track of time. I was reading Carson's acceptance from Harvard, which was pinned next to the emergency phone list and a photo of Carson with his parents and a gorgeous girl I didn't know, hiking on a mountain, wide smiles across all their faces.

"Hey," Carson said, behind me.

I jumped, startled and caught.

"Thanks for the soda."

"Sorry, I was just . . ."

"Yeah, I see," he said, opening the fridge and getting himself a can of soda. "So?"

"What?" I asked him.

"You tell me, you're the one going through my stuff."

"Harvard uses nice paper for its acceptances," I noted. "And who's this?"

Carson glanced at the photograph. "Me," he said.

"And?"

"And my parents and my sister Veronica," he said. "She's at Brown, a junior. What else?"

"Are you mad at me?" I asked.

He shrugged.

"Why?"

"Nothing." He pressed up against me and we made out a little. "I can't wait to get you alone, a whole weekend of freedom in the mountains. You want to go, don't you?"

"I have to ask my parents," I said.

"I'm asking *you*," he said. "Not your parents. Do you want to go?"

I hesitated, thinking for a sec, *Do I want to go?* I might have a party scheduled for one of those days, I couldn't remember, I would have to check on my Tallulah calendar, and anyway, what would my parents say if I even asked them, *Hey, can I go away for the weekend with my boyfriend?* . . .

"I knew it," Carson said, backing away from me. "I am so stupid."

"What? I just, I think I have a party scheduled that weekend, and anyway I'm not sure my parents . . ."

Carson shook his head. "Forget it." He walked out of the kitchen past the garage door to another room and slammed the door. I followed him, opened the door, and found him sitting against the laundry machine. I closed the door behind me and sat down next to him. "What's wrong?" I asked him.

He wouldn't look at me. "Nothing. I can't do it anymore, Josie, that's all. Everything I ask you, you say no. You toy with me like I'm a mouse and you're a kitten just having some fun."

"No," I said. "How can you say . . ."

"It's true. I thought maybe you were just scared, you have this incredible vulnerability under all your independence and strength and that's part of what turned me on, turns me on, but, I don't know. Maybe you're too young. Maybe I'm an idiot for . . ."

"For what?"

"For telling Frankie I think I could, I could, fall in love with you."

"You told him that?"

He looked at me. "I told him I'm falling in love with you, Josie. Isn't that stupid?"

"No," I said.

"Yes, it is," he said. "He said I hardly knew you, how could I be falling in love with you, I was just horny, and I punched him for it. It's not lust, I was telling him, it's this, connection, we're connected, me and Josie. There's a word my grandmother uses for it: *Beschert*. Meant to be."

"Beschert," I said.

Carson shook his head. "He thinks that's idiotic. But you know what I think?"

"Tell me," I said. *We are beschert, we are meant for each other.*

"I think it's stupid to fall in love with someone who isn't in love with you."

"How do you know I'm not?" I whispered.

"You're not," he said. "Everything I ask, you say no. Come to my house, come to the movies, come away for the weekend. All my friends will be there but my own girlfriend doesn't even want to come, doesn't even want to be with me!" He pounded the washing machine behind him with his fist. It didn't dent but it made a loud noise. It scared me.

"I just said I have to ask my parents!"

"Right. That's the first thing you said. I asked you if you *want* to come, you still haven't answered. Forget it. I have your answer." He shook his head. "You don't love me."

"Carson."

He wouldn't look at me. He studied his can of soda as if every answer might be printed on its side.

"Carson, listen to me."

"Forget it," he whispered.

"No," I said. "Listen to me. I have never felt this way before. You have me all riled up, and confused. I'm not used to feeling this way. Yes, it started out as a game, as playing, flirting, fun. That's all I ever expected it to be. But you know that flower you gave me?"

He didn't move, but I could tell he was listening to me.

"I kept it, Carson." I couldn't believe I was actually admitting this, but he was listening, and I was telling him, and it felt intimate, adult, right. "The petals started to turn black, on the edges, but I keep it in water, I change the water every evening, and bring it to my room. I fall asleep each night looking at that rose, and it's the first thing I see every morning when I wake up. It still has a little scent left in it, and I close my eyes and smell it and I think of you, Carson, and maybe you're right, maybe I say no to you too much. I'm sorry. Yes, you scare me. Not because I'm too young. Not because I hate you, though sometimes I wish I did. Sometimes I think, *Why did he have to change it, why couldn't we just hook up sometimes?* But then I realize how much I want to see you, be with you, all the time, how much I want to touch your fingers with my skin."

He looked up at me then.

"When you look at me, Carson, I know I belong to you. I know I'll do anything for you. I love you."

There. I said it. I waited, staring back into his eyes, thinking *Please say you love me, too.*

"No," Carson said. "You don't love me."

"How can you say that?"

"You don't," he said, standing up. "You don't love me. Forget it."

He started to leave the laundry room. I grabbed him by the arm. "Why? How can you say that? I left my best friend on his birthday. I broke his heart, to be with you here today, because you asked me to. What do you want from me?"

He pulled his arm away from mine. "Go back to him, then."

"Carson, why are you doing this?"

"Do you really?" he asked. "You really think you love me?"

"Yes," I said. I tried to hug him, but he didn't bend to me.

"I thought maybe you did," he said. "I brought you here, everybody was like, really, a tenth grader? Who dresses up like a clown and runs away from you? But I was like no, you don't know her. She's the most extraordinary girl, mature and real and unlike anybody I've ever known. I think I'm falling in love with her. I've been making an ass of myself."

"No."

"I . . . God! I sang to you. In the locker room! I have never sung in my life to anybody, not since fourth grade. I made a fool of myself for you. Following you around like your little mouse, toy with me, toy with me. But I was wrong. God help me, I thought I loved you, and I thought you loved me."

"I do," I said.

"No," he said. "You don't love me."

He stormed out of the room, almost ripping the door off its hinges on his way out. It swung open and shut in his wake. I stood there alone in the laundry room for a few minutes, trying to figure out what to do next.

And then I knew.

I went to the bulletin board in the kitchen and found a pen, hanging by a string, and an envelope with an old invitation left over from New Year's Eve. I crossed out the address on the front and wrote Carson's name in big letters. I turned over the envelope and inside, in the white space under the flap, I wrote:

Yes. I do.

Then I reached up to my ear and for the first time all year, unfastened my great-grandmother's diamond stud from my ear. It was beautiful, perfect and round and glittery, the most beautiful and valuable thing I have ever owned. Half of a perfect pair. I screwed the back onto the post and dropped it into the envelope. I sealed it shut and stuck it, with a pig magnet, to the front of Carson's refrigerator. I grabbed my jacket and left quickly, before I could change my mind.

Nineteen

LUCKILY MY MOTHER doesn't look at me all that much so she didn't notice the missing earring. I had sweated in her yellow sweater so I hid it in my bottom desk drawer, to deal with it during the week, because she and my father were home by the time I got back from Carson's. No lights were on at Michael's house, but I figured that meant nothing; he was probably still watching the movies in his room and his parents were probably still at work. I considered going back over there but decided against it. He had made it pretty clear he didn't want to see me, and before I could deal with him, I figured, it would be better to find out where things stood with Carson. I didn't even want to call Zandra or Tru. I got in bed and read, to escape my life.

My stomach was churning so much I couldn't eat dinner Sunday night or breakfast Monday morning. My mother seemed pleased. Maybe all the stress will be good for me, at least in my mother's opinion: my jeans were practically falling off. "Why aren't you eating?" she asked me.

I just shrugged.

"On a diet?"

"Sort of," I said.

"Ooh, which? I need a new one."

"May I be excused?" I asked, and brought my plate to the sink and went upstairs. I didn't think the high-stress-personal-turmoil diet was exactly what they'd print in the pages of one of her magazines.

I woke up early and washed my hair and even blew it dry a little, before trying to braid it. It didn't work. My fingers were shaking too much. I did a ponytail, as smooth as I could make it, and did my makeup slow and careful, a softer look than my usual dark lines, even curling my eyelashes. Carson hadn't come over after the football game, so I had to figure we were probably history, but I wanted to look better than ever so he could be sad over what he was losing, at least.

So? I tried to be objective, checking myself out. Should be easy to be objective, I thought—there is so much to object to. No, no, what I like best about myself is my flawless beauty. Well, my flawed beauty. One earring down, I looked off-balance, on top of all the usual stuff. I vowed not to cry through my non-waterproof mascara. I sniffed my flower and stood up straight. I am a strong girl, I told myself. I can handle this. I love him; I am willing to sacrifice half of my most valuable possession to let him know it. He doubted me, and who could blame him? He was right. I've been holding back. I hadn't let him know how I feel, so of course he eventually had to pull back and protect himself. He'd made himself vulnerable to me. He may look strong and confident but inside he was clearly feeling scared. How many people get to see that side of Carson Gold, the Golden Boy? I am the only one. He let me in, and I played the tease. What a jerk I am. I hurt him.

I have to show him that I love him.

I have to be strong, I told myself, at the bus stop. Michael wasn't there. I guess he got his mom to drive him. Maybe he didn't want to face me. Well, I told myself, his feelings are not my responsibility. I am in love with Carson, and Michael will have to cope with that.

I crossed my fingers like a baby the whole ride to school, praying please, Carson, forgive me. Please give me another chance. Please love me.

Relationships are work, I told myself. Am I afraid of work? Well, I am lazy, it is true, about most things, but on the other hand I am not always afraid of hard work. Am I? No. I work hard at something. What? Writing song lyrics. Ugh. At least I did. Will Michael and I stop writing songs together now? I guess so. Oh, Michael. No, Josie: focus. What was I convincing myself of? Oh, right, that I am not afraid. Of hard work. That was it. Well, also, I built my Tallulah the Clown business from nothing, from doing magic tricks for the kids down the street three years ago into a real job; I have already made almost a thousand dollars. Guests almost always ask for my number while I'm cleaning up, telling me what a great job I did. I am only a mediocre magician, but I run a good party and I work really hard at it. I like to. So if I'm happy to work at becoming Tallulah the Clown, I can certainly work at becoming Carson's girlfriend, right?

It's just different makeup.

I smoothed on some extra lip gloss, stalling at my locker. I smoothed down the pink sweater I was wearing for the first time, the tight, light pink sweater my mother had bought me for my birthday despite the fact that I have not worn light pink since kindergarten when I stopped being her dress-up doll and started wearing black stuff held together with safety pins. It's a costume, that's all. The black stuff, the pink stuff, the Tallulah multicolor stripes—it's all just costumes.

"Whoa," Zandra said when she saw me. "What have you done to yourself now?"

"That's pretty funny coming from you," I said, nodding at her newly green hair. "What did your mother say to that?"

"She called my shrink again," Zandra said. "Emergency meeting this afternoon."

"And you're going?"

"I'm turning over a new leaf," she said. "Therapy could be fun, I'm thinking."

"Holy . . ." Tru stopped in her tracks and stared at me. "I

thought Zandra was talking to a BP! Josie?"

"Overreact much?" I turned away from their stares to spin my combination. "How about her hair?"

"What?" Tru said. "Roy G. Biv. G for Green. We did it yesterday. But what is this getup for? Oh! Is this all for Carson?"

"Obviously," Zandra said. "How'd it go yesterday? Hey, where's your earring?"

I opened my lock and then my locker. On the shelf was the envelope I had left for Carson, with the address crossed out and his name on it. He was giving it back. "Oh, no."

I grabbed it off the shelf and tore open the envelope. Out fell his car keys. Not my great-grandmother's earring but Carson's car keys. I picked them up and uncrumpled the envelope, looking for a note. Nothing. I ripped it open some more. There was my note, my *Yes. I do.* He hadn't written anything back.

"What is it?" Tru asked.

I held up the car keys.

"What does it mean?" Zandra said.

"I don't know."

"Maybe he's giving you his car."

I pushed her on her forehead. "I don't think so."

"Did you have a fight with him?" Tru asked.

I nodded, trying not to cry. "Yesterday."

"Did he break up with you?"

I shrugged.

"Why didn't you call us?" Tru asked.

"Behind you," Zandra whispered.

I spun around and there was Carson. "Hi," I said.

He started to unbutton his shirt.

"Carson, what are you . . ."

There was a string tied around his neck, making a loose necklace. He gripped the string with his finger and thumb, and pulled up my earring, which was hanging by the back, from the string. He stood there holding it.

"What are you doing seventh?" he asked.

"You, maybe," I managed to say.

"Bring my keys." He slipped the string back into his shirt and buttoned up. Then he slung his arm around me, kissed me on the mouth, and walked me away from my friends, to homeroom, as everybody turned to watch us pass.

Twenty

CARSON MET ME before lunch, and we went out to the courtyard. Emelina pulled a small pink ball out of her bag and all the guys cheered. What a hero she is. I sat down on a bench, warning myself not to pout. *I could bring a ball sometime, that's not a big deal*, I thought. *I could definitely bring a ball, if that's such a great thing. I could bring a Wiffle bat. Wouldn't that be fun?* Luckily, Margo sat down beside me on the bench before I could work myself too deep into a funk. She really is very nice. I like her, despite how pretty she is. She complimented my sweater, asked me where I got it. I didn't know. She checked the tag and said it was from a really cool store. She was impressed that my mother is in advertising and very glamorous; I didn't tell her about the fart account. When the bell rang, Carson ran over to the bench red-cheeked and out of breath, and he put his arm around me to walk back into school.

Seventh period, I got to the back exit before Carson, and had my usual brief panic that maybe he was blowing me off. I have his keys, I reminded myself. He's going nowhere without me.

When he showed up, he kissed me, a nice slow make-out kiss, right there in the back hallway, just as the bell was ringing. "Hello, boyfriend," I said.

He flashed me his smile, took my hand, and led me out into the cold. At his car, he held out his hand. I put my hand in it. "The keys," he said.

"Oh," I said, and handed him the keys. What a dope I am. Did I think I was just going to plop into the driver's seat and drive his car, instantly? I walked around behind the car, settled into the passenger seat, and turned on the radio, looking for a good song while the car warmed up.

"How about . . ."

"What?" I asked him.

"Maybe just some quiet, today, okay?"

I turned off the radio. "Okay." I sat back and buckled my seat belt. "Are you mad at me?"

"No," he said. "Stop asking me that." He pulled out of the parking spot. "We won't do reverse today, but pay attention. You want to press the clutch before you shift, and ease the . . ."

Honestly, I was just listening to his voice, rather than his words. He glanced at me from time to time, so I nodded, but

I was busy memorizing his beautiful profile. I love you, I said silently to him. You don't have to be afraid anymore. I am yours. I love you.

He made the turn into my development.

"Oh," I said, with a fake laugh. "I thought, I mean . . . I thought you were going to teach me how to drive. But, that's okay. You don't have to . . ."

"Josie . . ."

"I'm not complaining," I quickly assured him. "You want to go, you know, explode some eggs? Ha, ha?"

"No."

"I was, it's a joke," I said, smiling so he'd understand. "I meant, we could just go fool around, in my room. That's fine." I was sweating. I put my hand on his thigh.

He stopped the car. "I'm going to teach you to drive, remember?"

"But . . ."

"So chill, okay? There's no traffic here, so you can go slow."

"Oh," I said. "That's fine. Sure. That'll be great." My teeth were chattering. It was a pretty cold day, despite my full-body sweat. Maybe I was nervous. Maybe I was scared witless. He was getting out of the car and so was I. I touched the dent on the roof of his car for luck, as I always did, and walked around the front. He kissed me as we passed each other. I got into the driver's seat for the first time ever, illegally, only fifteen. I could be arrested and go to jail. What if I did it wrong? What if I wrecked his car? What if he thought

I was an uncoordinated loser?

Emelina can drive a truck.

True, she ripped the top off it, but then she drove it topless four hours into the mountains. How is it that she does a total destructo thing that if I did, it would make me seem like a bumbling idiot, and she comes off as this sexy, powerful, independent, capable hero, and everyone in the room is left with the word "topless" on their lips?

I buckled my seat belt and turned the ignition key. The car was already on, apparently, judging from the grinding, squealing noises that came from both the engine and Carson.

"Sorry." I dried my palms on my jeans.

"Do you remember what I said about the clutch?"

"Yes," I lied, then admitted, "Well, no. Could you review?"

Following his instructions I pressed down with both feet and released the emergency brake. "It would be easier if you could see what you're doing," I said, trying to get a peek under the steering wheel.

"Keep your eyes on the road," Carson said, keeping his own eyes straight ahead. "Now move your right foot to the right and press . . ."

"This reminds me of dance class," I said, "Which I should admit that I failed. . . ." We were rolling forward. "Not that you can actually fail ballet, but I faked a sprained ankle and even though I couldn't keep straight which foot was supposedly injured, the teacher was so relieved, she . . ."

"Press the gas lightly," he interrupted. "Remember what I said, ease down with your right foot and up with your left. . . ."

"See what I mean?" My feet were doing what he told them to, like they had little foot minds of their own, while my mouth chattered on. "Right, left, up, down, it's like doing the hustle. . . ."

We were heading straight for Michael's hedges.

"You want to steer," Carson suggested. "Remember how to brake?"

"Yes," I lied. I knew there was something you had to do before you brake, he had been saying it right while I was admiring the angle at which his nose came from his forehead. He had said, what was it? There is something you have to do before you press the brake. Very important. You have to do something; don't brake until you press something. What? I grabbed a wand sticking out beside the steering wheel and pressed it, then slammed on the brake, just as we crashed hard into Michael's hedge.

It was apparently not the thing I was supposed to have pressed. In fact it activated the windshield wipers. If it had suddenly started to rain, pressing that wand might have been a good move. The sky was bright blue, however, as I could see over the edge of the bushes into which I had driven Carson's car.

"Put it in neutral," Carson said quietly. "And pull up the brake. The emergency brake."

I did what he said, then asked, "Are you okay?"

"I'm fine. Can you get out of the car?"

"Yes." I'm not sure if he meant would I be able to open my door despite the bushes or was I injured or was I such a disaster that I could not even operate the door handle, but I just opened the door and tried to get out. I failed. I then unlatched my seat belt and successfully got out of the car.

Carson was looming above me, waiting. When I was out of his way, he slipped into the driver's seat. I stood on Michael's lawn. Carson backed his car out of the hedge, which was only slightly dented, and thumped the car down off Michael's lawn onto the street again.

There were red streaks, like bloody scratch marks, striping the hood of his car. While he turned off the car, I reached over to touch the damage.

"It's just the red things," I assured him quickly. "Those red juicy bush-berries. It's washable. It's not blood. I mean, obviously, it's not blood. What I mean is I can fix it. I'll wash it. I'm sorry."

"Stop," he said.

"No, I insist." I tried to put my arm around him, to comfort him. "I'll wash it. You can just, if you pull it into my driveway . . ."

"That's fine," he said, stepping away from me. "I'll pull it into your driveway. Then I am going to take a walk, okay? I need to take a walk."

I nodded. "I'll wash it while you walk. Carson?"

He was getting back into the car. He stopped with one leg still on the pavement. "What?"

"I'm sorry."

"Okay."

"You forgive me?"

"Yeah."

"I love you," I said. He pulled his leg into the car and slammed the door. He drove the twenty yards or so to my driveway, and I walked along behind him. He was getting out of the car by the time I reached my driveway. "I'll have it shiny clean," I promised, smiling broadly at him.

"Half an hour," he said. "I have to get back for practice."

I watched him walk his brisk, long-legged walk down my driveway, away, and then ran inside to look for a bucket and sponge. He could have said, "That's okay, let's go to the car wash together." He could have said, "It's my fault, too, I shouldn't have pointed the car straight at a berry bush for your first time ever behind the wheel." He could have put his strong arms around me and said, *"Oh, Josie, are you okay? That's all that matters to me. Don't worry about the* car—*I love you, Josie."*

But maybe that's not fair. Maybe I am being unreasonable and selfish. I just drove his beautiful white car straight into a berry bush—did I really think he should be nice to me, comfort *me*, at that point? He has every right to be angry. His parents would probably be homicidal if he came home with his car so wrecked.

I found some sponges but no buckets. Where would we

keep a bucket? I bet Carson's family would have a bucket. I got the biggest of my mother's red pots. What the heck, they should get used, right? I filled it with hot soapy water and lugged it out to the driveway, and started to scrub.

Oh, Carson. I am sorry. You have every right to be angry at me. Why am I such a clod?

If Emelina drove his car into a bush, would he make her wash it?

That's not fair. Emelina is not his girlfriend anymore, anyway; I am. I am his girlfriend. I have to try to be good at it. If he wants me to talk a little less, is that so much to ask? And wear my hair in a ponytail? I could learn to braid. He thinks I have a beautiful face, is why he wants me to wear it that way. He wants to get a word in edgewise. I am an only child; maybe I am spoiled. Maybe I need to be brought down a notch.

That's not even what he's doing, I chastised myself as I scrubbed his car. I am such an exaggerator. He loves me, he chose me, he wants to see my face, he wants me. He wants to know I want him, and also, please, for me not to be so jerky all the time.

Is that so much to ask?

The berry stains were gone. I kept going. By the time he came back, I was sweating again despite the cold, clouds of breath puffing from my mouth as I shined every bit of his car to a gleam. "Hey," he said. "Hey." He caught me by both arms and pulled me close. He kissed me soft and tender. I dropped the sponge and wrapped my arms around him. He kissed my empty earlobe.

"Sorry," I said.

"Shh," he answered. "Forget it. I gotta go."

"Don't you want to come in?"

"I can't." He pulled away and opened the car door.

"I was asking if you *want* to," I said.

"Yes," he said. "But . . ."

"Yes," I said, too.

"Yes, what?"

"Yes, I'll go to Emelina's. Her mountain place. The weekend after next. With you."

He kissed me again, I closed my eyes and pressed against him.

"What about work?"

"I have a party," I admitted. "But I can cancel it."

He kissed me, soft and deep, then pulled back enough to ask, "What about your parents?"

I shrugged. "It's not up to them. We're meant for each other, right?"

He nodded and kissed me again.

"So, we should be together."

"Yeah." We made out for another minute. "I gotta go," he said. "I'll call you."

"Tonight?"

He slammed the car door shut and backed fast down the driveway. I stood there on my lawn, damp and soapy, and watched him go.

He didn't call.

Twenty-one

"DO YOU BELIEVE in *beschert*?" I asked my mother, as I was climbing onto the table and lying down.

"Never heard of it," Mom said. "Hold still for Bitsy."

"I believe in beeswax," Bitsy said. "Wow, have you ever had these eyebrows done before?"

"No," I said, closing my eyes. "Does it hurt?"

"It hurts to be beautiful," Mom told me.

Bitsy rubbed some warm, sticky wax over my right eyelid. *Not so bad*, I thought. It's kind of nice, actually. Maybe I am just tougher than most women, and don't make a big deal out of nothing.

Then she ripped it off.

I screamed. I said a bad word or three. Dozen. When I calmed down enough to do anything other than feel the pain of having my eyelid practically torn from my head, I noticed that my mother was laughing.

Not just laughing—she was cracking up. Poor Bitsy had backed into a corner, terrified, but my mother was sitting on a folding chair, practically gasping for breath, doubled over with laughter. How sick is that?

I watched her, amazed. No wonder I'm so screwed up: My own mother finds my pain hilarious. I truly have never seen her laugh so hard.

When she was able to lift her head and wipe the tears from her eyes, I said, "I'm happy I finally got a smile from you, Mom. If I had only known, I would've broken my arm when I was younger. That would've been a riot, huh?"

"What are you talking about?" Serious, suddenly. Ah, I was embarrassing her publicly again.

I shrugged. "I'm outta here." I jumped down from the table.

"You can't go, Josie," Mom protested, and actually stood up to block the door. "Show her the mirror, Bitsy."

"You're insatiable, Mom," I protested. "Is my pain really that funny?"

"Oh, for goodness' sake, Josie," Mom said. She grabbed the mirror from Bitsy. "Don't be so operatic! I was laughing at your vocabulary, not your *pain*. Look."

I looked in the mirror. She was right, I couldn't go. One of my eyebrows was curved like a movie star's, though red underneath. The other looked like a huge fuzzy caterpillar taking a nap on my face. I flopped back onto the table.

As Bitsy tore the wax off my left eyelid, I came up with another choice few words. Mom held up the mirror again. "Better, right?"

I shrugged, but yes, I looked better. I followed Mom out into the main room of the salon and into a small closetlike room, where Mom handed me a smock. "Put this on so your new sweater won't get wet while you're getting shampooed," she instructed.

"Is that really a verb?" I asked. "Shampooed?"

She rolled her eyes and shoved me toward the sinks. *I never should've agreed to this whole thing*, I thought, on my ways. Forget agreed—I had asked her to take me. You would've thought I'd given her a new cashmere sweater, from her reaction. She even almost forgave me for the one I'd ruined, after I asked to have my hair cut by an actual professional. How was I supposed to know that cashmere can't be put in the washing machine? Anyway, she was happy, and took the afternoon off work to bring me.

I sat down in the chair and was pushed back into a weird and uncomfortable position with my neck bent back over the cold lip of the sink, but as soon as the warm water hit me and Bitsy's hands began massaging my scalp, I felt myself relax. I closed my eyes and let my mind wander.

Carson. I couldn't close my eyes without thinking of Carson, his gorgeous face, his red, perfectly formed lips, his strong, slow hands. He'd been driving me home every day, lately (no more driving lessons); when we got to my house, we'd head straight up to my room to fool around. We were going farther than I've ever gone before, but that's okay, I told myself—he's my boyfriend, I love him, and he's a senior. I can't expect an eighteen-year-old boy to be happy just kissing with a little groping every day. When I told him I was a virgin at Frankie's on Saturday night, he said he knew, but he didn't say if he was or wasn't. Probably not. Probably he and Emelina . . . but I didn't want to think about that.

He wasn't pressuring me to do anything. Definitely not. Even if he was sometimes abrupt in how he talked to me, he was always gentle and slow physically. He was full of compliments on how I looked, and if he got annoyed when I talked too much, well, who could blame him? I do talk too much. I was trying to shut up more. I wrote SU (for Shut Up) on my palm with a Sharpie, to remind myself. Anyway, things were going well. Really well.

Except with my friends. Zandra and Tru had a "talk" with me on Sunday. They are "concerned" that I am "losing" myself. I assured them that I knew exactly where I was. They didn't look convinced. Maybe we're just growing apart. Maybe they're right that I haven't been such a great friend lately but I have other stuff going on right now and I wish they could just be happy for me. Michael meanwhile has been completely avoiding me. I put some of my stuff in Carson's locker so I wouldn't have to face Michael so much at my own. Carson walked me from class to class with his arm around me; those moments made the whole day worthwhile.

I craved them, did anything I could think of to get back in there, under that wing.

He is such an amazing combination of strength and vulnerability, my boyfriend. Maybe we're alike in that way. Maybe I had to test him, with all my teasing, and now it's his turn, sometimes. I have to show him I can take it, I can take his sarcasm and his moods. I'm strong. I've always been a strong person. I can take it.

And it's not like he's even so tough on me, really, at all. I'm just new at this, I think, and so I'm sometimes paranoid. When he sees me down the hall and his whole face lights up, I feel so good, I feel—what? Complete. Like there's nothing else I have to accomplish. I look back on all those days I spent arguing philosophy and dissing the high school experience with my friends, and I'm embarrassed about how immature I seem to myself, and how insecure. I had to put on this whole intense façade to prove I wasn't lonely—and now? Now I'm not lonely. Now I am Carson's girlfriend. People smile at me, and guess what? I smile back. Because life is good and I am where I belong, in the thick of it.

And then we go to my house and he smiles at me, touches my face, tells me I'm beautiful. And for those few minutes, I dare to believe it's true.

Sitting in front of another mirror in the haircutting chair, I listened to my mother's voice as she gave Bitsy instructions. Bitsy and my mother picked up pieces of my hair and looked, chatting, evaluating, not noticing particularly that there was a person under the hair situation.

"Can I go away this weekend?" I blurted out. There. Finally.

"Away?" Mom asked. "No. Where?"

"I don't know, the mountains. To a friend's grandparents' house."

"Which friend?"

Pieces of my hair were falling on the floor as Bitsy snipped her scissors briskly.

"Emelina."

"Never heard of her," Mom said. "With Zandra and Tru?"

"Zandra and Tru aren't friends with her."

"But you are?"

"Yes," I lied.

"How about Michael?"

"No," I said.

"But boys are going?"

"Yes." I turned my head. Bitsy *tsk*ed at me so I turned back to the mirror.

"Carson Gold?"

"Yes. Why are you quizzing me? I am not a baby anymore, Mom!"

"You weren't a baby when you were a baby," she said. "What's going on with you and him?"

"He's my boyfriend," I said. "Shocked?"

"No, actually."

"Forget it," I said. *I know you are shocked, deny it or not, because he's gorgeous, and a senior, and going to Harvard, and drives a white sports car. And you think I'm a loser. Admit it or don't, Mom. I know what you think.*

"I had a feeling," Mom said, smiling a little.

"We're in love," I yelled. Everything in the salon stopped for a second. Clearly I had an audience. "I'm in love."

"Congratulations," Bitsy said.

"Thank you," I answered. "My mother thinks he's too good for me."

"Is he?" Bitsy asked.

"Why would you say that?" my mother demanded—not denying that's what she thought—just asking why I would call her on it. Very tricky, Mom.

"He probably is," I told Bitsy. "That's why you have to make me as pretty as possible, to compensate. Right, Mom?"

"He wants to take you away for the weekend?" Bitsy asked.

"Yes," I said. "No. A bunch of people are going, it's not like that. It will be like ten of us, plus this girl's grandparents. But I'm probably the only one whose mother is making a big deal of it."

"Are you making a big deal of it?" Bitsy asked Mom.

"I don't need to," Mom said, throwing up her hands. "Josie's doing it for me. I didn't say a word."

"No way you'll let me go," I said. "I can't believe it. I shouldn't even have asked you. I should just run away."

"Don't cry," Bitsy said. "You eyes will swell and right after the waxing, that's bad."

"Do you want to go?" Mom asked me, irrelevantly.

"Why would I ask you, if I didn't want to go?" I asked.

"I'm not sure," Mom said.

"Okay," said Bitsy. She put down her scissors and her comb, and picked up a blow-dryer. "Put your head between your knees, like you're trying not to throw up," she said.

"Good idea," I said. For a minute I just let the sound of the blow-dryer drown out all my thoughts. When I was allowed to flip back up, my hair was off my face and Bitsy was pulling it hard with the brush, to dry and style me. I felt like Fluffy and Sarge must feel, which made me think again of Michael. It had been a week and a half, the longest I've gone without talking to him since I lost my baby teeth.

"You're thinking of letting her go?" I heard Bitsy ask my mother.

I couldn't hear what my mother answered. She met my eyes in the reflection and said something else I didn't hear. And then I noticed myself in there, in the reflection, beside my mother. I looked different. My hair was smooth and shiny, falling soft around my face, the ends just skimming my shoulders. It looked like a vaguely pretty girl but nobody I specifically recognized. I watched some expressions pass over the face of the girl in the mirror, and when we smiled at each other, Bitsy shut off the blow-dryer. "You like it, huh?"

She tucked the side hair behind my ear. My mother

stepped closer, then grabbed my empty earlobe, pinched it and yanked. "Your earring! Oh, no! My grandmother's diamond earring. It must have fallen out!"

The whole salon erupted into furious activity, everybody checking my one remaining earring, searching the sink, the garbage, the mess of hair in the dustpan. It all happened too quickly for me to stop them, and then it was too late to correct the misperception. By the time we left, the owner of the salon was so relieved to get rid of us, he refused to let Mom pay for my day of beauty at all, and promised to call her immediately if the earring turned up. Mom and I walked glumly to her car.

"Sorry," I said.

"Was the back on properly? You have to take care of valuable things, Josie. You always . . ." She shook her head. I didn't defend myself because the truth was way worse than what she was mad about.

She backed out and as we waited our turn to pull out of the shopping center's parking lot, she asked, "So you and that gorgeous boy are in love, huh?"

"What's so bad about that?"

"Nothing. It's wonderful," she said. "Isn't it?"

"Yes."

"So why do you seem so unhappy?"

I looked out my side window. She drove for a while, without talking for once.

"Your hair looks good," she said.

"*Beschert*," I said. "It means meant for each other. Do you think you and Daddy were meant for each other?"

She bounced her glossy lips against each other. "Meant for each other?"

"You don't seem it," I said. "I mean, you're all about how you look, he's a schlump; all he thinks about is feet, and all you wear is stilettos. . . . How come he doesn't bug *you* about your shoes?"

"Relationships are work," she said. "And they all have their miseries."

"Miseries?"

"Mysteries," Mom said. "I said mysteries."

"You said miseries."

"Josie! Why are you always looking for a fight?"

"I'm a pacifist!"

"So you say."

"Fine, forget it. Can I go this weekend or not?"

"Daddy and I will discuss it."

"Daddy will agree with whatever you say. He'll say, 'As long as she wears the orthotic shoes for her falling arches I don't care where she goes.'"

Mom laughed.

"Is that a yes?"

"I guess so," Mom said.

I looked at her, as she drove. Yes? "Really?" As easy as that?

She smiled. "I trust you."

"I'm supposed to do a party that weekend but I can cancel it, no problem."

"If you're willing to cancel a party for it," she said quietly, "it must be really important to you."

"It is," I answered. "Thank you."

Her pocketbook started to ring. "My phone. Quick. Josie! Get that for me. Come on, why are you always so slow?"

I found her phone in her bag and handed it to her. She flipped it open and started talking a mile a minute. Work. "No," she was saying. "Absolutely not. Well, tell him the sketches have to be in by Thursday or the . . . what? That's ridiculous, I don't care if the flooding is up to his armpits, I still need . . ."

"Mom!"

She was swerving a little, yelling into the phone, and almost sideswiped a car passing on our left.

"Ack! Don't yell, Josephine, you almost made me get in an acci . . . what? No, my daughter. I had to take her to a, a, a doctor's appointment. No. Fine, I'll be at a computer in twenty minutes, email me what you've got." She hung up and tossed the phone in my lap.

"It's dangerous to talk on the cell phone when you drive," I told her.

"You sound like your father. Listen, that reminds me . . ."

"Don't say I have to wear the orthotics."

"No, don't. They're hideous. Wear stilettos; that's what

they all love. Even your father."

"What?!"

"Nothing." She blushed a little. Weird. "No, I mean the lie I just told about the doctor's appointment. What about birth control?"

"Mom . . ."

"Please tell me you're using protection, and I mean condoms plus something else—are you on the pill?"

"I'm not using anything, Mom." *I am only fifteen years old. I'm in over my head as it is and I am nowhere near needing birth control.*

"Josie! You have to use something," my mother screeched. "Are you an idiot? Not using anything? That's suicide!" She turned to look at me and the car lurched into the other lane again.

"Mom!" I grabbed onto the door handle for dear life. "Please watch the road or you'll kill us today, before I ever get the chance to lose my virginity!"

"Oh," said Mom. "You're still, you're not . . . oh. Okay."

"Disappointed?" I asked her.

"No! That's good. Phew. I just thought, I mean, he looks so, grown up. So big."

"Mom!"

"What? I mean, usually you hang around with Michael, or Zandra and Tru. You just haven't had a lot of experience and Carson Gold seems like a, like he'd want you to . . . Phew. Okay. Good. Only Josie? I don't want to lecture you."

"But . . ."

"Not that you'd listen."

"I wouldn't," I agreed.

She gave a snorting little laugh. "Your hairstyle may change but . . ."

"Some things won't," I finished for her. "No."

"All I'm saying is, go to Planned Parenthood with a friend if you won't let me bring you to my doctor. Maybe this new friend, Alabama."

"Emelina," I said.

"Whatever," said Mom. "Does she drive?"

"Definitely," I told her.

"Fine. Get her to take you. If you're going to do adult things you have to be adult about them. Sex is serious stuff, and I don't mean just intercourse, either."

"Mom!" I felt like my brain might explode. "Stop talking! I told you I'm not even doing it."

"When you start having sex, Josie, you have to protect yourself."

"Don't you always?" I asked.

"Always what?"

"Have to protect yourself?"

"What are you talking about, Josephine? You know how it all works, right?"

"Yes, Mom," I groaned. "I was being metaphorical."

She sighed. I know she thinks metaphorical is a synonym for annoying. But then her hand moved toward me. I thought for a second she was going to hold my hand or something, so I held very still.

She just adjusted the heat. It would've been weird if she had tried to hold my hand, anyway.

Twenty-two

ON THE WAY up in the car, I turned to Carson and said, "So I cancelled the party I was supposed to do this weekend."

"Josie does birthday parties," Carson told Margo and Frankie, who were, as usual, making out in the backseat.

"Children's birthday parties," I clarified. "I'm a clown, you know, magic and everything."

"We know," Frankie said, coming up for air. "Remember? At the Eagles game?"

"Oh, yeah," I said. That seemed like two lifetimes ago, a different girl.

"You canceled a party this weekend?" Margo asked.

Carson reached over and squeezed my leg, left his hand there, heavy and warm. Good.

I turned around to talk to Margo. "It's a kind of funny story," I said, hoping it was. "The girl's name is Daisy Dang."

Margo smiled. I took a breath and reminded myself to talk soft.

"She's turning five years old on Saturday, and they'd been planning on me for a month. Her parents had ordered a $100 clown cake made with my likeness on it, from a photo taken at Daisy's best friend's party in October."

"Wow," Margo said, encouragingly.

So I continued. "Yeah. Mrs. Dang cried when I called to cancel."

"Mrs. Dang cried?" Margo asked.

I nodded. I liked playing the Emelina role. Carson's eyes stayed on the road but Margo and Frankie were leaning forward. I continued even a little softer: "Daisy Dang's father called me later, vowing to email every person in a fifty-mile radius with a child under ten and tell them how I had broken his daughter's heart. He said the extent to which he was going to ruin my business would match how badly I had ruined his daughter's birthday. He asked what I could possibly be doing that would justify my breach of contract and trust."

"Whoa," Margo exhaled. "What did you tell him?"

"What could I?" I checked Carson's face. He seemed to be enjoying the story, too. "I just told him something came up. He said I should be ashamed of myself."

"And are you?" Carson asked.

"No," I said.

I watched for his smile, but it didn't come. Why? I sunk

down in my seat, thinking *Great, now Carson is probably angry at me.* Maybe the story wasn't funny. Maybe it came off sounding boastful. *Oh, I hate myself,* I thought.

Margo and Frankie went back to breathing heavy in the backseat. They obviously have sex with each other. *Maybe that's what I need to do,* I thought. Maybe that would solve the problem. Am I really ready for that? I am only fifteen! Not that I thought I would necessarily wait until I got married but, I mean, one of my best friends hasn't even kissed anybody yet. The other, well, even Zandra hasn't gone all the way. Carson and I have gone farther than I'd ever gone with Michael—touched each other everywhere, shirts off, pants on. But having sex is a whole different thing. How far would I be willing to go this weekend?

I should have called Zandra and Tru to discuss it with them. I just didn't feel like I could. That made me feel lonelier than anything. I would have to figure this out alone. Fine, maybe that's good for me. Nobody was talking to me in the car anyway so I had plenty of time to talk to myself.

I love him, I told myself. If you love somebody you will do anything for him. If I love you, Carson, will you love me? Should I do everything with you? I have never been naked in front of anybody since I stopped wearing diapers. What would it feel like to be naked with you?

I watched him drive in silence. "What are you thinking about?" I asked.

"Huh?" he asked. "Nothing."

I sat there in lumpy silence, wishing he would sweep me off my feet again, like in the beginning. What if he is already getting bored of me? What if I am getting bored of him? Yeah, right. But clearly I had done something wrong, to be getting this silent treatment from him.

"Sorry," I said, feeling ready to cry, to offer to be dropped off on the side of the road with my suitcase and cell phone, to call my mother to come pick me up and listen to her tell me all the way home that I should never have expected Carson Gold to love me.

"Sorry for what?" He glanced over at me.

"For whatever I did wrong," I said.

"Did you do something?"

I shrugged. "Why are you not talking to me?"

"I'm just driving." He moved his hand from the gearshift onto my leg. "Do you like snowmobiling?"

"I love it," I said.

He shot me a look. "Have you ever gone snowmobiling before?"

"No," I said.

He smiled. God, I hate his smile, I love it so much.

"Hey," Frankie piped up from the back seat. "Are we going to that rib place tonight for dinner?"

"Yuck," Margo said. "Why don't we pick up pizzas, like when we came in the summer? That place was great."

"Maybe I'll make my famous chili," Carson suggested.

"Ew, not again," Frankie said.

"Have you had his chili yet, Josie?" Margo asked.

"No," I said.

"Lucky you," they both answered, cracking themselves up. "Let's go out, please," Margo begged.

I was really happy I had put all my money in my wallet, just in case. I wasn't sure how the whole thing was going to work, and I really had nobody to ask.

"What do you think, Josie?" Carson asked me quietly. He rubbed my leg. "Ribs? Pizza? Chili? What do you want to do tonight?"

"You, maybe," I whispered. The one answer I knew I knew.

Twenty-three

Margo and I were sharing a room. She told me as we put our suitcases on our beds that during the night one of us would sneak into the boys' room. That way, both couples could have some private time. She said it casually, like, of course. I nodded like, of course, too, silently thanking her for not mentioning the fact that of the four of us coming into the house together I was the only one with a rolling suitcase instead of a duffel bag. Or the fact that Emelina's grandmother knew Carson so well. I wondered if that moment when Gingy wouldn't let go of Carson's hand and told him she had bought all the ingredients for his wonderful chili was as awkward for Daniel as it had been for me.

Emelina and Daniel, meanwhile, were downstairs with the rest of the group, some seniors who were friends with Emelina. I was pretty thankful to have Margo around. She was on teams, too, so they all knew her. Not that anybody was nasty or snide, in fact the opposite: Everybody was extremely friendly to me, all smiles and *Love your coat—is it vintage?* No, I had answered, just old. They all cracked up. Turns out I'm funny. I was trying to relax. These people were just nice and gorgeous, why should that repel me?

Margo used the bathroom first, then I went, and I have to admit I was relieved she was sitting on her bed waiting for me when I got back to our room. "Your hair is different," Margo remarked, as we went down the stairs.

"Last time I cut it myself," I admitted.

"Really? I liked it," she said. "This is nice, too, but that was more, you know . . ."

"Different?"

"Yeah."

When we got to the great room, everybody was playing poker. Margo sat on the arm of Frankie's chair. I kind of hovered near Carson, who was deep in concentration. He laid down a card and collected the pot of chips. "Yes!"

"Lucky hand?" Margo said.

Carson grabbed me by the hips and pulled me onto his lap. "Yes," he said. "Very lucky. Both of them."

So it was all okay, and I coasted on that for the rest of the evening. He felt lucky to have me there, and that made it all worth it. I helped him cut up habanero peppers and plum tomatoes for his chili, which really wasn't so bad (though I only had a little; if your mother works in the gas-relieving industry, you become wary of beans) and turned down a slice of pizza (for similar reasons). Carson wrapped his arms around me as I washed the dishes, and then snuggled with me under a blanket in front of the fire. I felt his fingers tracing the bottom hem of my sweater.

"Yawn," he whispered.

I yawned. He yawned. Soon everybody was yawning, stretching, mentioning how tuckered out they were and how they were looking forward to an early start.

"Everybody talks about teenagers staying up all night," Pops said, standing up. "You all go to sleep before we do!" He headed toward his bedroom.

"Or at least to bed," Gingy said, with a glint in her eye, and followed him in. "Sleep tight!" she called. "Emelina, I'll be in to give you a kiss in a little while."

"Okay, Gingy," Emelina said, grinning. "Let's go to bed. Who's coming with me?"

A bunch of guys raised their hands. Their girlfriends swatted them down. Emelina grabbed one of the girls and they went off to Emelina's room, holding hands. We all watched her go, then headed our separate ways. As I followed Margo into our room, I saw Carson lingering at the door to his and Frankie's. He was watching me. I slowed down, held onto the doorframe. We stared at each other for a minute, then went to our rooms to change, and wait.

Margo went to the bathroom with her cosmetic case and a little bundle of pajamas to change into. I sat on my bed and tried to call Zandra on my cell, for an ego boost. No service, not one single bar. I felt a little like I did the first time I went on a sleepover, when I was six and didn't sleep one bit because I felt a million miles from home. I reminded myself that I was fifteen now, not six, and it didn't matter that I was far from home. My parents had the address and phone number up here; Carson had written it down for me to give them on a plain white index card and I had taped it to the kitchen wall where we don't have a bulletin board. It's only two days. And two nights. I am fifteen years old! Anyway, there wasn't going to be an emergency. If there were, they could just call me at the number I left for them, if they can't get through on my cell phone. No problem. And I could always ask Gingy if I needed to call them. Which I wouldn't.

I pulled out my pajamas and sat in a yoga pose to calm myself down. I had brought the flannel pants with yellow duckies on them, and an orange camisole with a built-in bra. Not the most comfortable thing to sleep in but I thought a T-shirt might look too dumpy. When Margo came out of the bathroom in a pink tank top with little tennis racquets crossed above her left boob and matching shorts with "love-love" scrawled across the butt, I realized I may as well have packed the comfy T-shirt. My stuff wasn't the right stuff anyway.

She sat on her bed with crossed legs.

I knew I should shut up and go to the bathroom but I hesitated. "Can I ask you something?" I asked her, redundantly.

"I need a, sort of a, girlfriend lesson."

"Sure," she said, tucking her hair behind her ears.

"Um, so, you're in love with Frankie, right?"

"Yes."

"How do you know?"

She thought about that for a minute, then said, "I'm happier when I'm with him. I'm stronger, more daring, more open. You know how when you're ten, you are so much who you are? When I was ten I was like the senior of being a kid. I was into sports, of course, but I was also into politics, I read the paper, I organized a recycling drive, I did cartwheels just because I felt happy. Didn't you?"

"Well," I said, "I have never done a cartwheel. Maybe I've never been that happy."

"No, you know what I mean. I was strong. And then in middle school I don't know what happened exactly but I kind of got scared. I was tense a lot, and I started watching the other girls more than the news. And me—I used to inspect myself in the mirror, agonizing over every flaw."

"You have flaws?" I asked her. "You're perfect."

"My eyes are too close together, my lips are like a duck's, one of my ears is pointy . . ." She showed me. It was true. "Please. But the thing is, when I started going out with Frankie, he liked my pointy ear. I used to hide it all the time, in fear that somebody would see it. He calls it my elf ear. I don't know." She flopped down on the bed. "And he needs me, too. He has never said the words *I love you* to anybody but me. He doesn't decide anything without asking me, because he trusts my judgment so much. Even about college. Well, partly because I'll apply early wherever he goes. He's my best friend."

"Wow," I said.

"When I'm not with him," she went on, the words rushing out of her, "I think about him all the time—what he would think, or say, how he would calm me down and help me roll with it, with whatever. And when I'm with him, it's just—easy. This might sound weird, but I'm more like I was when I was ten. Minus the cartwheels, plus a little, you know, different kind of physical stuff. I guess I know I'm in love with Frankie because I'm more like myself when I'm with him."

"Sounds like love," I admitted.

She flipped onto her stomach and looked at me. "How about you, with Carson?"

Before I could answer, there was a very faint knock on the door. She jumped up to open it and let Frankie in. "Hey, elf," I heard him whisper.

I picked up my pajamas and my cosmetic bag. "Bye," I said, on my way out. I don't think they heard me. In the bathroom I changed, brushed my teeth, washed my face, and reapplied a little bit of mascara. I wadded up my clothes and shoved them, on top of my cosmetic case, into a corner between the sink and the bathtub. Sneaking down the hall to Carson's room, I heard the floorboards squeaking like cannon booms.

The door opened before I knocked. Carson was standing in a white T-shirt and white boxers and his ragg-wool socks. He pulled me into the room and kissed me, his arms closing the door behind me and then wrapping me up, pulling me close. We kissed standing there in the middle of room for a few minutes, until he pulled gently away. He took off his T-shirt. There was my earring, still hanging from the string around his neck. I touched it with my finger. He took my finger and kissed it lightly, then pulled me gently toward the far bed.

I followed him, but when he sat down, I stayed standing. He pulled gently on my hand, and said, "What's wrong?"

"Nothing," I whispered.

"Don't be scared."

"I'm not." I started lifting the bottom of my camisole, edging it above my belly button, taking my time. His eyes flicked from my belly to my eyes and down again, and when they didn't come back up, I turned around and let him watch my back as I pulled the camisole off. I turned my head to make sure he was still watching.

"Oh, Josie," he said.

"It's all coming off," I whispered, crossing my arms over my chest. It was absolutely freezing in there. "I want to be completely naked with you."

"Yeah?"

"I love you, Carson."

He didn't say anything.

"Do you love me?" I asked. "Tell me you love me."

"Josie," he said.

"What?" I was starting to shiver.

"Come on. Come here. You're shivering."

My teeth started to chatter. "That's a no? You don't love me?"

Carson stood up. I scrunched down on the floor and grabbed my camisole. "Josie, why are you doing this? Come on. Do you want to fool around or you want to fight?"

"Say it," I said. "Say you don't love me."

I watched his feet, so near my head, in their adorable socks. His toes gripped the floor and then relaxed. "I don't love you."

I pressed my camisole against my naked chest. "Why did you drag me up here? Do you know what I did for you?"

"Not the martyr routine again." He walked away. "I asked if you wanted to come. Whatever you did, you did for yourself, not for me. Don't blame me for your choices, Josie. I mean really. Grow up."

I swallowed. He was right. "But I love you," I said, my voice sounding weirdly strangled. "What am I supposed to do with that?"

I didn't wait for his answer. I dashed out of the room with the camisole pressed against my naked body, praying nobody would be in the hall, and ducked into the bathroom. With the door locked, I pulled on my camisole, and then my sweater from my pile of clothes. I climbed into the cold, dry bathtub and had a long silent cry.

When I was all cried out, I looked at myself in the mirror for a while. Then I sat on the closed toilet, trying to plan my next move. It was Friday night and I was stranded in the Poconos, with no way to get home, and nobody to love me. He doesn't love me. I considered crying about that all over again but I guess I was done.

If Carson comes to the bathroom, I will forgive him, I decided. I can't make him love me. I don't really even need that. I love him. That could be enough, and maybe eventually he'll love me. Less than two weeks ago he said he thought he could fall in love with me. Maybe what he meant tonight was that he doesn't love me yet, that he needs more time. Obviously. And I was rushing him. I was pressuring him.

I am such a jerk. Why am I so pushy? I don't need to forgive him; I have to ask him to forgive me! What did he do wrong? I asked him a question and at least he respected me enough to answer honestly. Most boys would've been like sure, whatever, I love you, keep taking off your clothes. Not that I'm such a prize, naked, but if you believe some people, boys don't care. Well, but that's not true, I don't think. Michael wouldn't say he loved me just to get me naked; he just loves me. And Carson could've, but chose not to. Did I want him to lie? I should go apologize for freaking out like that, for rushing him, for blaming him. I should beg him to start the night over, fresh.

But I can't go back in there, I thought. I will not be that girl chasing him around. No, not me, no way. *Maybe he's gathering the courage to come back in here right now,* I thought. Maybe he'll make some sort of grand gesture to show me he may not yet love me, but he is now teetering on the edge of falling in love with me.

I stood up fast and washed my face. He could be in here any second. No swollen eyes! Yuck! How could he love me when I look like a monster? I filled the sink with icy water and plunged my face into it. I stayed in there holding my breath for as long as I could stand it, then did it again and again until I had a headache. I dried off and applied my makeup as carefully as I could, curling my eyelashes, smudging on just a subtle bit of shadow.

Beside my feet was Margo's cosmetic case. I opened it. Yes, lip gloss. I used some and put it back carefully. She wouldn't mind, probably, I told myself. She's so nice. Frankie loves her. They're best friends. Why aren't Carson and I best friends?

When I was as good as I could make myself look, I sat down on the toilet to wait. I allowed myself to check my watch only at five-minute intervals, telling myself if I checked in under five minutes, I would jinx it and he wouldn't come.

After half an hour I started considering the possibility that he wasn't coming anyway. After an hour I washed the makeup off again. My face felt raw from so much scrubbing in one night. I crawled into the bathtub and pulled the

shower curtain closed. There were frighteningly lifelike pictures of goldfish on the liner, and a white terry curtain outside. I counted the goldfish to keep from being scared or sad.
I got lost in the sixties a few times but kept counting until,
eventually, as the light started coming in through the
window above my head, I fell asleep.

Twenty-four

I WOKE UP to the sound of water running, with no idea where I was. It took maybe two seconds for me to figure out that

a) I was in the bathroom,

b) in the tub,

c) not alone, and

d) that was not water running.

When I heard the toilet flush my theory was confirmed. What to do? If I said something, the person who just peed would be at least startled if not furious, and I would have to explain what I was doing fully dressed in the tub. I resolved to lie very still until the person finished washing his or her hands and with any luck that would be the end of it.

Clearly I was not having a lucky weekend. A hand, a boy hand, reached behind the shower curtain and turned on the water. The bath started filling. I was getting damp. *Think,* I thought. I needed a plan. The hand felt the water, adjusted it a little warmer, and turned the middle knob so the shower went on. I had to do something; the situation was only getting worse. When I saw the hand grasp the shower curtain, I realized that in about one second a naked boy was going to step onto me in the bathtub and most likely have a heart attack on the spot.

Think!

As reassuringly as I could, I said, "Don't panic."

Unfortunately, the clatter of the shower rings skidding across the pole and the thrumming of the water into the tub (and onto me) must have drowned out my voice, because Daniel, fully naked, lifted his leg to get into a tub I was lying in, unintentionally taking his shower.

"Stop," I said, calmly, at the exact second, or maybe a split second after, he saw me.

He screamed. I screamed. I'm not sure why I screamed. I was startled, too, I guess, even though I'd had some time to prepare myself. It was a startling situation. He pulled the shower curtain closed between us but honestly it was too late. I had seen it all by then.

"What the hell are you doing in there?" Daniel yelled.

I decided I may as well turn off the water. "Taking a shower, apparently."

He didn't respond for a minute, and then said, "But . . . I turned on the water."

"True," I said. I stood up. Water dripped off me. My clothes felt extremely heavy.

"So you weren't in the middle of your shower, when I came in."

"Right again," I said, wringing out my hair. "No wonder you got into Princeton. You're a junior?"

"Sophomore," he said.

I smiled at the goldfish pictures. "Oh."

"Josie?"

"Yeah."

"Okay," he said. "I'm going back to my room. When you're done in here, leave the door open."

"Okay," I said, and then, since I couldn't resist, added, "Nice seeing you."

After the door closed, I opened the shower curtain again and stripped off my clothes. I grabbed a towel off the pile and scampered back to my room. Margo was gone and the beds were tightly made. I got dressed quickly and rubbed my hair dry. I was determined to be bright and fun, easy to get along with, smooth like Margo, confident like Emelina.

When I got down to the great room, Frankie and Margo were in the kitchen, trying to be subtle about watching Carson and Emelina, who were at the table, playing cards.

"Good morning," I said, smiling brightly.

Nobody responded.

"Queen of spades," Carson said, slapping a card onto the top of the pile. "I'm doomed."

Emelina raised one eyebrow at him.

"You're asking for it," Carson said. He slapped his hand down.

"Bull," Emelina answered, low and sexy.

"Oh, yeah?" Carson asked, leaning close to her.

"Hey, Josie! Want some eggs?" Frankie offered. "I'm scrambling."

"Sure." I was relieved to hang with them in the kitchen, getting the butter, the salt, anything to keep from looking toward the table, until the eggs were done and plated. Carson and Emelina had just finished the game when we got out to the table. I sat down beside Carson and started to eat my eggs, without tasting them.

Margo picked up the cards. "Whose fortune can I tell?"

"Mine," Frankie offered.

"Okay." Margo smiled and shuffled, then started laying out cards as her eggs cooled. "Three cards here, four there, and I'll do me at the same time."

Frankie grinned up at her.

"Okay," Margo said, considering the cards. "For you, I see a young love. You run away together."

"I hope yours says the same."

Margo tilted her head. "No, mine says I'll fall in love with somebody old and rich and he'll die and leave me alone, but very, very wealthy."

Frankie pushed the cards away and said, "I'll kill him."

She grinned at him and took a bite of her eggs.

"Do mine," Carson said.

"Okay." Margo swallowed, shuffled, and laid a new array of cards on the table. "Let's see, diamond, spade . . . hmm, I don't know. I messed up." She reached to sweep up the cards. Carson grabbed her hand and stopped her. "No," he said. "The cards don't lie. What? I die young or something?"

Margo didn't answer. "It's just a game," she said, her voice quavering. "It doesn't mean anything."

"Let go of her arm, man," Frankie said.

Carson let go, shoved his chair away from the table, and went to the front door. He stomped into his boots, grabbed his jacket from the coat rack, and went outside. Emelina stood up.

"Go," Margo whispered to me.

I jumped up and followed Emelina to the door.

"I'll go," I said to Emelina, as we sat on the bench beside each other, putting on boots.

She stopped lacing hers up and considered me.

"You still love him, don't you?" I asked her.

"Yes," she said.

"Does he still love you?"

"Yes."

I swallowed hard and grabbed my jacket off the hook. "What about me?"

Emelina shrugged.

I shook my head. "No. That's not fair."

"Fair? You think it's a game?"

"No," I said. "I don't."

I pushed out the door into the cold morning. It had snowed a ton overnight. The cars looked like massive marshmallows. Everything was white. I clomped through the knee-high powder until I found Carson around the side of the house, sitting sideways on a snowmobile.

"Hey," I said.

He looked up at me. "Hey."

"Want to go for a ride?"

"Sure," he said. "But I'm driving."

"Deal."

He got on and I sat behind him, pressed against his back with my arms hugging his waist. He turned it on and we started flying, fast and smooth, into the fields behind the house. He took a path through the woods and we went awhile like that. It was absolutely beautiful back there, the trees heavy with snow and no noise but the roaring of the snowmobile's engine and the pounding of my heart. When we emerged we were on the far side of a pond, beyond which I could see the house, covered in snow, smoke billowing out of the chimney. It looked as peaceful and pleasant as a scene could look. Carson headed toward the house, around the lake, but three-quarters of the way there he hit the brakes and stopped. He turned off the engine.

I didn't let go of him, and he didn't release the handles. We just sat there for a few minutes in the quiet.

"You should never have come," he finally said.

I rested my head on his back.

"I shouldn't have made you come. This isn't your scene, these aren't your friends. You're miserable and so am I."

"I am not," I said, though my tears were dripping onto his jacket. "I'm having a great time."

"No, you're not." He pried my hands off him and turned his head toward me. "I think we need to end this before either of us gets hurt."

"Too late!" I yelled. "I'm already hurt. How can you do this to me? You begged me to be your girlfriend. I told you it wouldn't work but you convinced me. And now, when my heart is wrapped up, when I have given up everything to be your girlfriend—my friends, my job, my clothes, my . . . everything! Everybody is mad at me and now you're just like, oh, sorry, never mind? What the hell is that? I am turning myself into a pretzel to be wherever you want, whenever you want, whoever you want, and you just throw me away like a piece of trash?"

"I guess you were right," he said, calmly.

I shoved him off the snowmobile. He landed on his back in the snow. "Love is a brat, you think? No, love is fine. You are the brat, you spoiled, rotten brat!"

"Josie . . ."

I stood above him. It took all my self-control not to stomp his gorgeous face with my boot. "I love you!"

"Josie!" Someone was yelling my name, far away. "Josie!"

I turned and looked toward the house. Frankie was

standing there in just his long johns, waving his arms. "Come here! Come in!"

I squinted toward him and saw the back door open. Michael walked through it. Michael? Michael! I started running toward the house, leaving Carson on the ground behind me.

Twenty-five

"MICHAEL!"

I got to the back deck out of breath and grabbed onto Michael's jacket sleeves.

"I tried your cell," Michael said. "I tried it like a hundred times."

"There's no service up here," Emelina said, coming out of the house, too, in her boots and coat. "Notorious."

"And the phone lines are down, so . . ."

"From the storm," Emelina explained. "Gingy was just saying we got almost fifteen inches."

"What's wrong?" I asked Michael. "What happened? What are you doing here?"

"It's your mom, Josie."

I kept my grip on his olive-green sleeves and didn't move.

"She was in a car accident."

I felt my knees buckling under me.

"She's in the hospital. She's pretty banged up, couple of broken ribs and a black eye, your father said, but she's okay."

Emelina dusted the snow off a chair. "Sit down."

I did. I looked up to thank her and saw Carson, beside her. Michael knelt in front of me. "She wants to see you," Michael said. "Your father called me. He gave me the address. I said I'd bring you right away."

"Michael."

He took my hands. "She'll be fine, Josie. I promise. Come." He stood up and pulled me. I stood up too but didn't take a step. "Come on, Josie."

I looked at Carson. "You want me to go."

"Of course," he said, in his soft soothing voice. "Your mother was in an accident, Josie. What are you gonna do? Stay here and bumper ski with us? Go!"

"You want me to go so you can be with her." I pointed at Emelina. By now most of the people were on the back deck, but I didn't care. "You want me out of the way so you can get back together with Emelina." I turned to Daniel, who was leaning against the back door. "You know that's what's happening here, don't you, sophomore?"

"No," he said. "I have no idea what's happening here. I'm having a surreal day."

"Don't you care that your girlfriend loves another guy?"

Daniel shrugged. "High school drama."

"Josie," Michael said.

"I'm not going," I told him.

"You have to," Michael said. "Josie, come on."

I broke away from him and went to Carson, threw my arms around him. "Come with me," I begged. "Please. Carson, I love you. You love me, don't you? You did. You almost did. You were falling in love with me, remember?"

Somebody stop me, I thought. I am that girl, that horrible girl screaming *But I love you Carson!* But even recognizing that I had become my own worst nightmare, and knowing then the complete humiliating futility of pleading, begging, screaming in front of everybody, I couldn't stop. "Frankie!" I turned on him ferociously and saw him flinch. "Didn't Carson say he was falling in love with me?"

Frankie shrugged his bony shoulders.

"He did! He told you. Carson," I was crying, yelling, smiling, everything at the same time. "Come with me. I need you to be there with me. It's not over between us, I swear it's not. Don't give up on us. I'm sorry for, for everything. Okay? Please. I love you! Don't you love me even a little?" I looked deep into his eyes, into his witch eye, hoping for some magic.

Carson pushed me softly away. "Go."

Michael picked up my hand. "Come. It snowed seven inches last night." He shot a nasty look at Emelina, then leaned closer to me. "The roads are bad. It'll take three hours, at least. Let's grab your stuff and get out of here."

"Carson," I said.

"Go," Carson said. "The guy drove up in a blizzard to get you, and your mother is in the hospital. What's wrong with you?"

"You, maybe," I said.

I let Michael lead me toward the back door.

Twenty-six

I SLEPT THE whole way home. I didn't think I'd be able to with all that was going on but I think I was asleep before we got to the highway. Michael woke me in the hospital parking lot. I blinked my eyes, looking at him, gradually remembering what had happened. "Hey," I said. "You drove."

He half-smiled. "I turned sixteen two weeks ago."

"I remember," I said. "I can't believe you drove up to get me in a snowstorm. Your mother let you?"

"She wasn't pleased."

"I bet." I could just picture that scene. "Why would you do such a stupid thing?"

"Tell you later." He unbuckled me. "Let's go in."

"Michael . . ."

"Later," he said.

We zipped through the parking lot and into the lobby.

I hate hospitals so much; they are way too full of sick and damaged people. We went around and around, down a long corridor, up an elevator, down another long hall, stopped at a nurse's station. Michael talked to them. I stared at my feet.

"Come on," he said, and I followed him to a door. He knocked and we went in.

My father jumped up, off the edge of the bed. He threw his arms around me. "Josie," he said, and then turned to Michael. "Thank you so much, Michael."

Michael shook his head. "I'll wait outside, to bring Josie home."

"Right, okay," Dad told him. "Good idea."

"Mom?"

She looked weird, a little dazed, banged up, and pasty. It was scary.

"You okay?"

"You look so worried, Josie," she said, and started to laugh, but stopped herself, grabbing her side. "Oh, don't make me laugh, that's the worst. Don't frown like that, Josie, or you'll be a wrinkled prune by the time you're forty."

"Well, that's a relief," I said. "If you're still criticizing me, you must not be that close to death."

"Death?" She started to laugh again but caught herself. "You are the most operatic person. I had a little accident. I'm fine. You should see the other guy."

"You hit somebody?" I hadn't even thought of that.

"Mom, you hit somebody? How is he? Were you talking on your cell phone?"

"No," she said. "And yes. The guy I hit was twenty feet tall and made of oak, or walnut, or something."

"You hit a tree?"

"It was the tree's fault," she said.

I smiled, a little. She smiled back.

"Hey," she said. "You're back already from your fabulous weekend?"

"It wasn't very fabulous," I admitted.

"Did you eat cheese?"

"No," I said. "Mom, I am more than a digestive tract."

"What happened to your hair?"

I turned to my father. "I gotta go," I said. "Are you staying here or going home?"

"Go," my mother said. "Come back in the morning and spring me from here."

"They have to see if the bleeding stopped," my father said to her, and then said softly to me, "She had a lot of internal bleeding."

I took a deep breath, trying to figure out what to do. It was habit to be mad at her, and she just pushes all my buttons, even from a hospital bed. Even with internal bleeding. Why couldn't she be like Michael's mother for once and tell me what a fine young woman I was becoming? Maybe if she did, even once, even if it were a lie, maybe I'd have a better chance at becoming a fine young woman.

Her eyes were closed.

"What's wrong with her?" I asked my father. "Is she okay? Did she just pass out? Maybe we should call a nurse."

"She's had quite a bit of morphine," he whispered. "She'll be fine, the doctors think. She was lucky." He couldn't take his eyes off her. Gently he brushed the hair off her forehead. I watched him, realizing it had been a long time since I'd seen them touch. "We were lucky."

"Do you like stilettos?" I asked him.

"What?" He was fussing with my mother's covers. "Oh, the high heels? They're awful. The worst thing for feet, absolutely dreadful."

"Mom said one time . . . something. Nothing."

He looked at me, finally, sheepishly. "That I liked them? Yes, well. Your mother has amazing legs, and they do look good in those awful shoes." He kissed her forehead. I looked away. If I were in a hospital bed, who would kiss me as I slept? Not Carson, probably. Maybe he would. Maybe he would realize he loved me, if I were in a hospital bed. But maybe not.

I would want him to be there.

"Why don't you head home," my father suggested. "I'll stay here again tonight, but I'll call you later. Or you can call here. Michael has the number. He's a good person, Michael."

"Unlike me," I muttered.

"No," Dad said. "Like you."

"That's not what Mom thinks," I said, and turned toward the door.

My father grabbed me by the jacket. "Don't. You. Dare. Don't you dare criticize her."

"I wasn't," I stuttered. "She always criticizes me. Why don't you ever yell at her?"

He shook his head. "Get out of here. Go." He shoved me toward the door. I slammed through it.

"Let's go," I said to Michael.

"You okay?"

I didn't answer, just started walking fast down the hall. I couldn't even see where I was going. I set the pace and Michael set the course, yanking me around corners and into an elevator. "Is she all right?" he whispered as the doors slid shut.

"She's the berries," I said.

Out in the parking lot, the cold air on my face felt good. I followed Michael to his father's car. He opened my door and closed it after I was in. We drove for a while without talking.

"They must've been cracking up when they brought her in," he said.

"Oh, yeah," I said. "A car accident with internal bleeding is a big laugh." I looked out my window. *I am alone in the universe*, I thought.

"No," Michael said. "I meant the clown getup."

It took me a minute to hear what he said. "The what?"

"They didn't tell you?"

"Tell me what?" I asked.

"That's where she was, or where she was going, when she got into the accident. They didn't tell you?"

"Tell me what, damn it, Michael?"

He made a complete stop at a stop sign, turned right, and pulled over on the side of the road. "You blew off a birthday party, Saturday?"

"I canceled one," I said.

"Apparently the mom of the kid called, asking if by any chance your plans had fallen through because they like hired a pony or something and the kid was still all broken-hearted, only wanted Tallulah the Clown. So, your mother—and this is third-hand, this is what your dad told my mom—your mom told this lady that you had to be out of town for a very important meeting but that your backup had become available, and would do the party."

"I don't have a backup," I said.

"Yes, you do."

"My mother?"

He nodded.

It was impossible to imagine. "My mother was going as my backup?"

"She was on the cell clarifying the directions when she smashed into a tree. When they brought her into the hospital she was in the rainbow wig, the striped suit, whiteface, red nose . . ."

"Was she driving in my clown shoes?"

"That I don't know," Michael said.

I hit myself on my forehead with the heels of both my hands. "She thinks it's that easy? You can just put on the costume and that's it, you become Tallulah? She doesn't know the first thing about doing it. She doesn't know how to run a kid's birthday party! Maybe it looks that easy to everybody else but there's a lot more to it than putting on a red nose, believe it or not. What the hell was she thinking?"

Michael shrugged. "Maybe she wasn't thinking anything. Maybe she was just backing you up."

"Why would she do such a stupid thing?"

"Why does anybody do a stupid thing?" he said. "Love. She loves you."

I opened my mouth to protest, but started crying again instead.

He sat there quietly for a long time while I cried myself dry. He didn't even look at me.

"Michael . . ."

He turned the car back on and said, as he pulled out, "Love makes us stupid, sometimes."

I looked out the window as he drove. "Thank you," I said.

Twenty-seven

"YOU HAVE TO stop stalking him," Zandra said to me Friday morning. She slammed my locker shut. "Come down to lunch with me. We'll annoy Tru while she tries to read."

"I'm not stalking him," I said.

She stared at me. "Josie."

"Okay, maybe I'm stalking him, but what else am I going to do?"

"Nothing," she said, looping her arm through mine. "Do nothing. He doesn't exist. Let's go."

"It's not that easy." I pulled my arm away. "You have no idea what Carson and I . . ."

"It's not a marriage, Josie," she said. "The whole relationship crashed and burned so fast I've only changed my hair color once since it started."

I smiled a little, but it turned into a sigh. "It's been a

rough week," I explained.

"That's why we're cutting you a lot of extra slack. But now your mom is home and on the mend and it's time for you to suck it up and move on."

"This is a lot of extra slack?"

Zandra nodded. "Yeah. But enough already. It's time to take out the stupid ponytail and put your own clothes back on. Come sleep over my house tonight with Tru. We'll watch sappy movies and mock what's-his-name while we eat junk food and paint our nails black."

"I don't want to." I spun the combination only Carson and I knew, and yanked open my lock. "He likes to see me, really see me. He thinks I'm beautiful. Crazy, huh? But for the first time in my life I don't feel ugly if my face shows. He did that for me. What you don't get is that I don't want to go back to how I was."

I opened my locker and bent down to get my stuff. Tru's sneakers were rounding the corner to stand beside Zandra's. Great. They were ganging up on me. I blotted my damp eyes with my sleeve and didn't look up at them.

"What you don't get," Zandra said, "is that your real friends don't actually care what you wear or do to your hair. That's not the point. We just love you, me and Tru. Right?"

"Right," Tru said. "And Michael, too."

"The jerk," Zandra said. "He's totally in love with you. We know you, and we love you, no matter what. So we deserve you. And the Golden Egg? Well, screw him. He blew it, his loss. It's time to move on. Say good-bye."

"Hey!" Tru pointed at my Wiffle bat as if it were infectious. "What the heck is *that*?"

I looked at it and said, as innocently as possible, "It's a Wiffle bat."

"Is there a Wiffle ball team you have joined," Zandra asked, "to complete your personality transplant?"

"Sometimes we like to play ball at lunch," I muttered.

"They," Zandra said. "Not 'we,' Josie. They play ball at lunch. You argue about philosophy. You don't play ball. You listen to cool music and help your friends and organize peace rallies, and you laugh. Loud. Remember you? You don't have to be a poor imitation of *them*. You are a fabulous, weird, original, smart, kind, strong person."

"I'm not weird." I stood up and faced them.

"Well, you're pretending not to be," Tru said. "And the effort is making you miserable, Josie. Look at yourself. You have dark circles under your eyes and what do you weigh now? Nothing? You really want to dull yourself down like this? For what? For a guy?"

"He's not just a guy." I rested my head against the cold metal of the locker next to mine.

"No," Zandra said, her hand on my shoulder. "He's a guy who, after maybe a week of being into you, has now clearly dumped you."

"He did not dump me!" I shouted. I grabbed the bat and swung it up in the air, to take aim at their heads.

Tru took a step back but Zandra didn't flinch. She stared at me, hard and cold, her lips tight.

"I'm his girlfriend!" I yelled.

Zandra shook her head.

My arms were shaking. "I love him."

"I know you do, Josie," Zandra said slowly. "But he doesn't love you."

"How can you say that to me?" I felt the tears well up in my eyes. "You're supposed to be my friend."

"I am your friend. That's why I'm telling you this," Zandra whispered, reaching up to take the bat from my tight fists. She placed it gently back inside my locker. "You have to try to stop loving him, because he doesn't love you."

Tru touched my shoulder. "Asymmetry sucks."

I pulled away.

"You know where we'll be," Zandra said.

I watched Zandra and Tru walk away from me. I knew they were probably right, but what did that mean for me, about me? That I was nothing? That once he got to know me, he decided, oh, yuck?

I sunk down against my locker, caught my aching head in my hands, and cried. They're right. He doesn't love me. I love him so much and he doesn't love me. Wait, what if they're wrong? Okay, Carson and I are obviously going through a bad time, but all relationships are work; my own mother said they all have their miseries, or even if she said mysteries—this week of him not talking to me might be a mystery of my relationship with Carson that my friends could never have access to. Just because we're in a rough patch, does that mean I should give up? It didn't even make sense: I'm being lousy to Zandra and Tru and they still love me, they were still trying to reach me, right? They weren't just writing me off, saying good-bye, moving on. No. They were sticking by me, showing me how much they love me. Isn't that what good friends do? And don't I love Zandra and Tru for that? Of course I do. So don't I owe at least that much being a good friend to my boyfriend?

Well, except that Carson and I were never really friends.

He just swept me off my feet, and here I am, on my butt.

I hoisted myself off the floor. He hadn't given me back my earring. He still had it, which meant he hadn't given up on us. Maybe he was taking some time to figure out how he felt, and giving me some time. My mother had just gotten out of the hospital, after all. Maybe he was feeling guilty about how badly the weekend had gone and was so embarrassed he wasn't sure how to approach me. People think he's smug and confident but they don't know him the way I do. I wiped my face dry, grabbed my lunch and bat, and headed away from the cafeteria, toward the courtyard.

He once loved how strong and independent and real I was, so that's what I should definitely pretend to be. Maybe he was testing me, seeing if I could handle the rough times, too; how can you make yourself vulnerable to someone, fall in love with her, until you know if she'll stick with you no matter what? He gets so much attention for his looks and achievements—but that's all earned love, in a way. That kind of love could disappear if his grades slipped or he got cut from a team or his face was horribly disfigured somehow. So maybe before he can fully fall in love with me is unconditional love. Isn't that the highest form of loving somebody? To love him unconditionally?

I had to prove to him that I could take it, that I was strong, that I would love him no matter what. I put down my lunch and Wiffle bat and sat on an icy bench near the gate that led from the courtyard to the parking lot. Even though I didn't fully believe it, I told myself: this is a test, it is only a test, a test of my love for him. Fine. I'm good at tests. I sat on my fingers to keep them warm, and watched the gangs of seniors heading toward me. Maybe today is the day I'll finally pass this test. Soon everything will be easy and equal between us at last.

Carson. I could see his walk before I could make out his features, his long strides, so confident and balanced. I sucked in my breath. As he got closer I could see his gorgeous face, and then my eyes were drawn down. His hand was holding Emelina's.

Twenty-eight

SIT STILL, I begged myself.

They came closer and closer. Maybe he will be embarrassed and drop her hand. Maybe he's just comforting her about something, maybe she bombed a test, or got her finger slammed in a door and he's just being a good friend. Don't I want my boyfriend to be a good friend? To his ex-girlfriend?

Well, no. I don't, actually.

I saw Margo see me, and Frankie. Frankie grabbed Carson's arm and whispered something, and then Carson glanced toward me. He didn't slow down, he didn't smile. He didn't drop Emelina's hand.

Stay still, I told myself.

I stood up.

Carson reached into his pocket and pulled out his car keys. He handed them to Emelina. "Why don't you pull my car around," he said to her. "I'll be right there."

"Okay," she answered.

"You sure?" Frankie asked him.

"Go ahead," Carson told them.

Margo tried to catch my eye, but I wouldn't look at her. I was staring at Carson.

"Hi," he said.

"Hello," I said.

"How's your mom?"

"Fine," I said.

"That's good."

"Carson," I said. "Listen, I know this has been a rough time. I'm sorry I've been . . . whatever I've been. I'm sorry. Can we just . . ." I smiled at him. "Let's start over, okay? Hi, I'm Josie." I held out my hand, to shake his.

He didn't take my hand. "Don't do this."

I kept smiling, determinedly. "Tell me what you want me to do. Anything. I'll do it, Carson."

He shook his head. My hand was still sticking out, between us. *Please,* I thought, *take my hand at least.* Touch me. Let me at least once more touch your fingers with my skin.

"Carson, I love you."

"It's over, Josie. I gotta go."

"You have to go to her? To Emelina? You're back together?"

"Yes."

I felt my fingers curling into fists. "Did you teach her to drive, too?"

"She taught me, actually," he said softly. "Come on, Josie. Let's end as friends."

"Friends?" I was yelling by now but I didn't care. "How can we end as friends? We weren't friends to begin with. My friends are inside, waiting for me. My friends care about me. They love everything about me. You and me—we were just hooking up. We were never friends."

"Don't say that," he murmured.

"We weren't. We were nothing, and then you twisted me up and made me fall in love with you. You're my first love, Carson. Don't I mean anything to you?"

He glanced toward the parking lot.

I shrieked. It was a scary sound. I think I scared both of us. "Look at me! Look at me! I am crazy. About you. I belong to you. You are the only thing that matters to me, not even myself, not my, I gave, I'd give . . ." My head was reeling. "I gave you my great-grandmother's earring. Don't you know . . ."

He nodded. "I have it." He pulled his wallet out of his back pocket.

Out in the parking lot, the horn of his car beeped twice.

"Coming," he called. "One sec!"

He opened his wallet and fished out a tissue with a tiny lump in it. He refolded his wallet, put it back in his pocket, and unwrapped the tissue. There it was, my great-grandmother's sparkling diamond, in his creased hand.

"No!" I yelled. "It's yours! I'm yours!"

"No," he whispered. "It's yours. You should keep it."

I picked up the Wiffle bat with both hands and took aim at his horrible gorgeous head.

"What are you doing, Josie?" he asked, smiling kindly. "Come on. I thought you were a pacifist."

"I've changed," I said.

"You planning to kill me with a Wiffle bat?"

"Yeah."

"Why?" he asked.

The bat was shaking in my tight grip. "Because I don't have my Minnie Mouse pillow," I said.

He smiled for real. Oh, man, that smile.

"Carson . . ."

His smile dimmed. He held out the earring to me in his open palm.

I smashed his hand as hard as I could with the Wiffle bat.

"Ow!" he screamed.

My earring went flying.

Carson was rubbing his red palm, inspecting it for damage. "That hurt," he shrieked. "You really hurt me."

"Right back at you," I said. "Good-bye, Carson."

He frowned, massaging his hand, the big baby. "I just wanted to end this nicely."

"Yeah?" I cocked the bat back up to hit him again. "Well, this time you don't get what you want."

He backed away from me, toward his car. The passenger door flew open. He turned and sprinted the last few feet, flung himself into the passenger seat, and slammed the door shut. They peeled out, racing away from me.

I didn't lower the bat or get down on my knees to search for my other earring—or cry—until they were gone. It took awhile but I didn't give up until I found it, under an old brown leaf. I stood up and put my earring back where it belonged. Then I chucked the Wiffle bat into a garbage can, wiped my eyes dry, and headed inside.

ACKNOWLEDGMENTS

First I'd like to thank my father, who made me practice saying, "First I'd like to thank my father" regularly as a child. He was so confident that someday I'd win a Tony for best play, he was already working on my acceptance speech. Especially because I don't write plays anymore, the Tony's looking increasingly unlikely—but for that unwavering confidence in me, thank you, Dad, almost as promised. Before I thank Dad, though, I'd like to thank Mom, my great friend and confidant who not only likes me just as I am but also still helps me to do so, too.

Abigail McAden and Amy Berkower are extraordinary partners and also quite wonderful lunch companions. Avi, Judy, Sarah, Chris, and Meg get me through the sludgy uphill parts of writing a book, for which I owe them deeply. Thanks to Julie Golin, who helped me figure out a bunch of details of life in PA, to Magda Lendzion for all she does every day, and to the good people of the Authors Guild for their tremendous support.

Despite all the real-life inspiration from people I know or knew well, readers who write to me so movingly about their own lives, and my own adolescent self, I want to be clear: This is a work of fiction. My resemblance to everyone in it is purely coincidental.

A special big operatic thank you to the Metropolitan Opera Children's Chorus, particularly Elena Doria, Alicia Edwards, and all Zachary's other friends at the Carmen Café and beyond. Though the genders are switched here, I hope some of the music remains. *Toi, toi, toi.*

To Mitch, Zachary, and Liam: You are the men I hope someday to deserve.

Rachel Vail

EXTRAs

You, maybe

Tru's Top 10 Favorite Books

1. *You, Maybe: The Profound Asymmetry of Love in High School* by Rachel Vail

It completely reminded me of this thing one of my best friends went through this year; weirdly true to life!

2. *The Fountainhead* by Ayn Rand

Anybody who stands alone, laughing, naked, on the edge of a cliff is either brilliant or seriously off, and definitely sexy.

3. *Pride and Prejudice* by Jane Austen

Smart, sexy, and romantic.

4. *Of Mice and Men* by John Steinbeck

Powerful story of friendship and sacrifice.

5. *The Princess Diaries* by Meg Cabot

Fast, fun, and funny—and you know you secretly imagine being Mia!

6. *The Sun Also Rises* by Ernest Hemingway

Totally romantic and intense, and in Spain, where it's *hot!*

7. *The Complete Works of Shakespeare* by you-know-who

Okay, the histories are boring but the comedies are seriously bawdy and the tragedies, well, it doesn't get deeper than this.

8. *A Separate Peace* by John Knowles

Another great friendship story, with boys but still good anyway, and I have a total crush on Finny.

9. *If We Kiss* by Rachel Vail

If I ever kiss for the first (and second, and . . .) time, I want it to be as romantic and hot as when Charlotte kisses Kevin (or George!).

10. *Atonement* by Ian McEwan

Meant for adults but he totally nailed the voice of the thirteen-year-old.

Zandra's Guide to Changing
Your Looks but Keeping Your Self

DO:

1. Hair today . . .

It's just hair. Do something way different! It can change both your looks and your outlook. Get a bob, dye a pink streak, attach a long ponytail. Don't stress if it's hideous. Even the most disastrous mistake grows out pretty quickly.

2. Change your clothes!

Again, go wild. I'm not talking bikinis in January. Self-preservation! But if you are usually goth, try something pretty and pastel, or vice versa. A funky jacket or a wacky pair of sneakers might make people (including yourself) look at you fresh. . . .

3. Make one thing up . . .

Choose a feature you want to emphasize. Eyes? Lips? Keep the rest of your makeup really simple (or skip it altogether) and go to town on that one feature. Maybe do big lashes this week. Next week, it's all about lip gloss.

4. Clean up

Body odor and dirty nails are gross. Wash, brush, start fresh. Nobody wants to work on a dirty canvas!

<u>DON'T:</u>

1. Buy into the hype!

Ew, who wants to let a bunch of old people on Seventh Avenue decide what looks good on you? Also, if it's totally in now, you will look way out of date in ten minutes. What do *you* like? Confidence is more gorgeous than any $$ jeans.

2. Put all your bread in the window ...

That's my grandmother's expression for someone who shows all her, ahem, assets as much as possible. Honestly, it does look cheap. A little mystery goes a long way.

3. Be a pincushion

What did you think was cute five years ago? Ten? Still love it? Please. Think about that before you let somebody draw a tattoo on you. Plus, they have to use needles—yuck!

4. Ditch your friends for a guy

You can change up what you wear to catch his eye if you really want to (though I never would!), but ditching your friends for a guy is always ugly. And if things don't work out with the guy, you'll be sitting alone on the curb with mascara dripping down your face—also not the most flattering look. Trust me—been there. If your mascara's gonna run (and it is, girl, someday it'll be you crying the black rivers), you'll need your pals to wipe your cheeks.

A Q&A with Michael

Q: How long have you been in love with Josie?
A: Who says I'm in love with her?

Q: Aren't you?
A: Well, yes. I guess. No. Forever.

Q: Why didn't you ever ask her out?
A: She was pretty clear about her feelings on that subject.

Q: What are your ambitions in life?
A: To be a musician. To save the world. To write the perfect song.

Q: What are you scared of?
A: Something bad happening to my parents, or disappointing them.

Q: Favorite food?
A: Red candy. Or sushi (not red).

Q: Bad habit?
A: Nail biting. Can't seem to stop.

Q: What is the worst thing you ever did?
A: Used a friend.

Q: Why did you do that?
A: Revenge. And I was stupid, all messed up. And maybe horny.

Q: When?

A: The weekend Josie went away with SuperBoy. Saturday night. 10 P.M.

Q: What did you do?

A: I will never tell, and neither will Zandra.

Q: Zandra?!

A: I completely deny anything happened with me and Zandra that night.

Q: Is that why you drove up to get Josie during a blizzard the next day? Guilt?

A: Guilt. Love. Stupidity. Insanity. Hope. Kind of a chopped salad of dysfunction, huh?

Q: Do you want to end up with Josie, after all that has happened?

A: No. Yes. Absolutely not. Maybe.

Rachel Vail on Her Inspiration for *You, Maybe*

AS I WAS WRITING my new book, *You, Maybe: The Profound Asymmetry of Love in High School*, the question in my mind was: What happens the first time love crashes over your head and pulls you in? What do you risk? What do you lose and what do you gain?

At the time, my son, Zachary, was ten, and performing in the Metropolitan Opera's production of *Carmen*. I was never much of an opera fan, I admit. I had always thought of it as, well, a bunch of fat people shrieking in foreign languages. But Zachary loved it, and there he was up on that huge stage, so what was I going to do? Buy a ticket and watch. Of course. And listen. And slowly—despite my resistance—the beauty of it started reaching me.

But still, it's true, my mind would wander. As I sat in my red velvet seat in the audience, I found myself, as always, working. Imagining. Bizet's music became the soundtrack inside the mind of this cool tenth-grade girl I was creating, as she fell horribly in love with a devastatingly charismatic guy.

During the seventh performance, I figured out why I was getting such good work done there. It wasn't just that I was trapped, unable to get distracted by e-mails and alphabetizing the refrigerator. It was much more fundamental: The opera *Carmen* was enacting the same story I was telling in my book!

I almost jumped up and shouted YES! But they frown on that in the opera house. Also one of my shoes had fallen off under the seat in front of me. I waited until the

7

intermission, fished out my shoe, and then ran to a café across the street to write, write, write. Those hours when the story comes fast and furious are the best part of being a writer.

There are, of course, big differences between *You, Maybe* and *Carmen*. Nobody is singing in the book, certainly not in French, and the story takes place in Pennsylvania instead of Spain. Also, in *Carmen*, it is the guy who throws his life away for doomed romance. Gender switch! The flirtatious, sexy Gypsy Carmen became, in my book, the magnetic senior hottie Carson; Don José, the star-crossed soldier, became smart, strong, fragile Josie Dondorff. Also, in mine nobody ends up dead. In place of a knife there's a waffle bat. But both are stories about losing yourself in love.

You may have fun going through and finding the many tricky little references to the opera—from settings to expressions. (Hint: Emelina is based on a bullfighter!) But you don't have to go there at all. Either way, I hope you will enjoy this story on its own.

It was horrible and exciting, equally, becoming Josie as I wrote her story. I wanted to explore, as part of a tale of first love, dealing with hook-ups (the friends-with-benefits issue, as well as the not-even-really-friends-just-giving-benefits issue) and questions of different kinds of love (parent/teen love, friend love, romance). As always, I have many more questions than answers.

There is so much that happened in the lives of every character in this book that is not contained in the text. As I create characters, I write short stories and sentence completion tests and diary entries for each of them, even the ones who have tiny parts in the main book. It's not efficient, but it is the best way I know to ensure that my characters are multidimensional and interesting. But then I can only include the stuff that propels the story along—so maybe 5% of what I write actually makes it into the final book. Sometimes even really juicy stuff doesn't get in. Is it any wonder I sometimes have to write a new book from the perspective of one of the characters in a book I just finished? This is why for my next project, I am writing a trilogy about three sisters the summer their wealthy, beautiful, seemingly perfect family falls apart—one book from each sister's point of view, so as you read, you find out more and more secrets they keep from everyone, even each other. . . .

For more on my books and how I write, as well as tips for your own projects, please visit my website. I'd also love to know your thoughts after you read *You, Maybe* or any of my other books. What would you have done in Josie's situation? Have you ever felt so overwhelmed by your feelings that you ignored your own best rational thoughts? I'd love to read your opinions.

Visit me anytime at www.rachelvail.com.

Quiz: How Good Is Your Crush?

JOSIE IS SMART, strong, and independent, but when she falls for Carson Gold . . . well, not for nothing is it called a CRUSH. Take this quiz to find out just how bad you've got it—or how good!

1. **When you see your crush, does your body freak out?**
   (a) My palms sweat, I can't remember how to breathe, speak, or walk, and my heart makes every effort to evacuate through my ribs.
   (b) No.
   (c) My stomach tightens and my fingertips go frosty.
   (d) I can't stop smiling and my cheeks and ears heat up.

2. **How do you feel when you spend time with your crush?**
   (a) excited, buzzy, nervous
   (b) bored, distracted, itchy
   (c) embarrassed, shaky, self-hating
   (d) relaxed, happy, confident

3. **Think of someone whose judgment you respect, who is totally on your side. What would they think of your crush?**
   (a) that we are a surprising match, but interesting, maybe
   (b) that I deserve better
   (c) that I should immediately delete his name from my phone, IM list, brain, and vocabulary
   (d) that we are terrific for each other

4. **If there is something I like to do that my crush is not into . . .**
   (a) I would just do it without him.
   (b) I would stop doing it.
   (c) I would pretend I am not, never have been, never would be into it.
   (d) I would be excited to tell him about it.

5. **If my crush is into something I am not . . .**
   (a) We're actually into a lot of the same things, but I guess I'd be like, fine, whatever, we're not supposed to be fused at the brain.
   (b) I would be all like, ew, you like that? And try to get him to stop it.
   (c) I would try to get into it, whether I like it or not.
   (d) I would ask him about it.

6. **When I daydream about my crush . . .**
   (a) I imagine things we've done together, but make them come out better by changing what each of us did and said.
   (b) It's hard to imagine us together, actually.
   (c) He's way nicer to me than he is in real life.
   (d) I fantasize about all the fun stuff we'll do together.

7. **When I see my crush talking with other girls, I feel**
   (a) a little vulnerable
   (b) homicidal
   (c) suicidal
   (d) eager to join the conversation

8. **What does your crush think about you?**
    (a) that I am hot
    (b) I have no idea if my crush thinks about me at all.
    (c) that I could lose a few pounds or talk less
    (d) that I am beautiful, funny, interesting, fun

9. **When we talk, it is usually**
    (a) just chatting about school, life, friends, thoughts.
    (b) We don't actually talk to each other.
    (c) criticism.
    (d) about things we have done or might do together.

10. **If my crush and I were trapped in a room alone together for an hour,**
    (a) we would both be pretty happy about it.
    (b) we would probably end up arguing.
    (c) we would both be stressed out of our minds.
    (d) we would wish for another hour.

11. **When I am with my crush, I act**
    (a) like myself, but tense because I am trying so hard not to mess up.
    (b) like I always act.
    (c) like the person I think he wishes I would be.
    (d) like myself at my most comfortable and best.

12. **If I could just somehow subtract my crushy feelings for my crush,**
    (a) I would recommend him to my best girl friend

as a great catch for her.

(b) I would like him as a buddy.

(c) I would have nothing to do with him.

(d) he'd probably be my best friend.

13. **The part of me that's most interested in my crush is:**

(a) my heart—I just have these amazing feelings for him.

(b) my head—I know we'd be good together.

(c) unable to admit in a quiz format—okay, it's major lust.

(d) all of the above.

SCORING:

Count up how many A's, B's, C's, and D's you answered.

If your answers are mostly A:

There may be something growing between you and your crush, but don't push. As you enjoy those weird tension-filled moments, don't let him pull you away from the other stuff you care about. Stay busy with friends, activities, everything that keeps you happy, productive, and sane. If your crush is a good match for you, all that stuff will draw him nearer. . . .

If your answers are mostly B:

Sounds like you are more interested in having a crush than in this particular crushable. That's fine! It doesn't have to happen now-or-never. A crush will womp you in the head when you least expect it . . . eventually! I promise.

If your answers are mostly C:

Though your heart may pound, anxiety does not equal love! If your crush is from afar, don't worry and enjoy! But if this is someone you are trying to have a relationship with, BEWARE! It is bad news to be into someone who is not good to you, or causes you more trouble than happiness. If you wouldn't take it from a friend, definitely don't take it from a crush. Get out.

If your answers are mostly D:

Sounds like you have a good healthy crush going. Yeah! Remember to keep your dignity and sense of self and then—have fun! Having a crush is one of the best parts of being alive . . . after, of course, having a crush on someone who has a crush on *you*! Good luck!

How'd you do? Any surprises? Can you guess how Josie would have scored? If you want to know how she did, or how Rachel scored on the quizzes—yes, she does test these things on herself—visit her website (www.rachelvail.com) and go to quizzes! She'd love to hear how you did, too!

Other Great Books by Rachel Vail

If We Kiss

Kevin led me quickly around the side of the building, then stopped. I managed not to crash into him. I tried to look calm, cool, unperturbed. I told myself not to laugh, especially not a snorting kind of laugh. "Wha . . . what did . . ."

And then he kissed me.

Charlotte (Charlie to her friends) falls for the one boy she can't have: Kevin. Why? Her best friend is in love with him. And Charlie's mom and Kevin's dad are dating. Still, Charlie can't help but wonder, *what would happen if we kiss?*

"Amazing what one kiss can do."—*Kirkus Reviews*

Do-over

Whit doesn't get girls, in either sense of the word "get." Especially his crush, Sheila. All he knows is that unlike in basketball, there are no do-overs in life—or in love. Which is either really scary or really awesome, depending on how you look at it.

"This is the real thing!"—*BCCB* (starred review)

Ever After

Instead of having the time of her life this summer, Molly has two best friends who are fighting, and her ex-fling Jason acting all weird. She's beginning to wonder if "happily ever after" really exists. At this point, she would just take the ever after part.

"A funny, desperate story."—ALA *Booklist* (starred review)